AYI KWEI ARMAH was born in Takoradi, Ghana, in 1939. He was educated at Achimota School, Groton School and Harvard University. He has worked as a translator, a scriptwriter for Ghana television, and in Paris as translator-editor on *Jeune Afrique*. He has also taught at the Universities of Lesotho and Wisconsin.

The Beautyful Ones Are Not Yet Born (1968) was the writer's first novel, followed in 1970 by *Fragments*, *Why Are We So Blest?* (1972), *Two Thousand Seasons* (1973) and *The Healers* (1978); all of these have been published by Heinemann in the *African Writers Series*.

AYI KWEI ARMAH

THE BEAUTYFUL ONES ARE NOT YET BORN

HEINEMANN

Heinemann International Literature & Textbooks
a division of Heinemann Educational Books Ltd
Halley Court, Jordan Hill, Oxford OX2 8EJ

Heinemann Educational Books Inc.
361 Hanover Street, Portsmouth, New Hampshire, 03801, USA

Heinemann Educational Books (Nigeria) Ltd
PMB 5205, Ibadan
Heinemann Educational Boleswa
PO Box 10103, Village Post Office, Gaborone, Botswana

LONDON   EDINBURGH   MELBOURNE
SYDNEY   AUCKLAND   SINGAPORE   TOKYO
PARIS   MADRID   ATHENS   BOLOGNA

© Ayi Kwei Armah 1968
First published in Great Britain 1969
First published in the *African Writers Series* as AWS 43 in 1969
First published in this edition 1988

ISBN 0–435–905–406

Printed in Great Britain by
Cox & Wyman Ltd, Reading, Berkshire

93 94 10 9 8 7

For
Mrs Dickson and Gwen

CHAPTER ONE

The light from the bus moved uncertainly down the road until finally the two vague circles caught some indistinct object on the side of the road where it curved out in front. The bus had come to a stop. Its confused rattle had given place to an endless spastic shudder, as if its pieces were held together by too much rust ever to fall completely apart.

The driver climbed down onto the road from his seat, took a crumpled packet of Tuskers from his shirt pocket, stuck a bent cigarette in his mouth, and lit a match. The head refused to catch, however; there was only the humid orange glow as the driver resignedly threw away the stick and took out another. After the third try a yellow flame sputtered briefly. The driver caught it quickly with the end of the cigarette before it died, cleared his throat and spat out a generous gob of mucus against the tire, and began unhurriedly to inhale his smoke.

Inside the bus the conductor took down his bag and slowly rubbed his neck just above the patch where the long strap had been pressing down. Then he sat down heavily with his legs dangling down the front steps and closed his eyes. The passengers shuffled up the center aisle and began to lower themselves gently down, one after the other, into the darkness of the dawn.

When the soft scraping of sleepy feet on the hollow metal of the steps had stopped, the conductor sat up, his eyes wide open, took his bag from off the floor, drew from within it his day's block of tickets and, laying this on the seat beside him, poured out all the money he had collected so far beside it. Then, checking the coins against the tickets, he began to count the morning's take. It was mostly what he expected at this time of the month: small coins, a lot of pesewas, single brown pieces, with some fives, a few tens and the occasional twenty-five. Collecting was always easier around Passion Week. Not

1

many passengers needed change; it was enough of a struggle looking round corners and the bottoms of boxes to find small coins somehow overlooked. So mostly people held out the exact fare and tried not to look into the receiver's face with its knowledge of their impotence. Collecting was certainly easier, but at the same time not as satisfactory as in the swollen days after pay day. There was not much in it at a time like that. True, people were still only bodies walking in their sleep. But what could a conductor take, even from a body that has yet to wake, when all this walking corpse holds out is the exact fare itself, no more, no less? Much better the days after pay day, much, much better. Then the fullness of the month touches each old sufferer with a feeling of new power. The walkers sleep still, but their nightmares in which they are dwarfs unable to run away and little insects caught in endless pools, these fearful dreams are gone. The men who dreamed them walk like rich men, and if they give a fifty-pesewa coin they look into the collector's eyes to see if he acknowledges their own import-ance. They do not look in their palms to see how much change is there. Much better the swollen days of the full month, much better.

The conductor separated the money into little piles and saw that there was not a single fifty-pesewa coin. No wonder. The coins had yielded nothing. He had not thought they would, but then sometimes a simple check like that could reveal hidden profit. It was not very likely though, that he would make any-thing from the coins today. There was something still. Some-one had at this time of the month held out a cedi for his fare. He had looked into the face of the giver, and sure enough, the eyes had in them the restless happiness of power in search of admiration. With his own eyes the conductor had obliged the man, satisfied his appetite for the wonder of others. He had not lowered his eyes: that would have brought the attention of the potent giver down to the coins in his palm, and the magic would have gone, and with it the profit. So the conductor had not lowered his eyes. Instead he had kept them fastened to the hungry eyes of the giver of the cedi, and fed them with admir-ation. He had softened his own gaze the better to receive the

2

masculine sharpness of the giver's stare. He had opened his mouth slightly so that the smile that had a gape in it would say to the boastful giver, 'Yes, man. You are a big man.' And he had fingered the coins in his bag, and in the end placed in the giver's hand a confusing assortment of coins whose value was far short of what he should have given. The happy man had just dropped the coins into his shirt pocket. He had not even looked at them.

The cedi lay there on the seat. Among the coins it looked strange, and for a moment the conductor thought it was ridiculous that the paper should be more important than the shiny metal. In the weak light inside the bus he peered closely at the markings on the note. Then a vague but persistent odor forced itself on him and he rolled the cedi up and deliberately, deeply smelled it. He had to smell it again, this time standing up and away from the public leather of the bus seat. But the smell was not his mistake. Fascinated, he breathed it slowly into his lungs. It was a most unexpected smell for something so new to have: it was a very old smell, very strong, and so very rotten that the stench itself of it came with a curious, satisfying pleasure. Strange that a man could have so many cedis pass through his hands and yet not really know their smell.

After the note the conductor began smelling the coins, but they were a disappointment. Not so satisfying, the smell of metal coins. The conductor started stuffing them into his bag, first checking everything against the tickets to make sure how much he had gained. He felt reasonably contented. It would, he hoped, be a good day for him, Passion Week or no Passion Week. Again his nostrils lost the smell of the cedi's marvelous rottenness, and they itched to refresh themselves with its ancient stale smell. He took the note, unrolled it this time, and pressed it flat against his nostrils. But now his satisfaction was mixed with a kind of shame. In his embarrassment he turned round, wishing to reassure himself that the bus was empty and he was alone in it.

A pair of wide-open, staring eyes met his. The man was sitting in the very back of the bus, with his body angled forward so that his chin was resting on the back of the seat in front of him, supported by his hands. The eyes frightened the conductor. Even the mere remembered smell of the cedi was now painful, and the feeling in his armpit had suddenly become very cold. Was this the giver turned watcher already? Had his own game been merely a part of the watcher's larger game? Vague fears of punishment drove their way into his mind. He had not thought it possible that so many different shapes of terror could come to him in such a little time. And now the crime seemed so little and so foolish and the possible punishments so huge that he could only pity himself. He was about to go down as the victim of a cruel game.

The watcher only continued to stare. He did not need to hurl any accusations. In the conductor's mind everything was already too loudly and too completely said.

'I have seen you. You have been seen. We have seen all.' It was not the voice of the watcher. It could not be the voice of any human being the conductor knew. It was a large voice rolling down and everywhere covering empty spaces in the mind and really never stopping anywhere at all. So this was it. The watcher. What could a poor man say to their voices? What was there to reply to tricks and the deception of the innocent?

And so words and phrases so often thrown away as jokes reveal their true meaning.

And Jesus wept. Aha, Jesus wept.

In his own moment of despair the conductor did not weep. He opened his mouth and uttered the fullness of his outrage. 'What?'

But, perched on his seat in the back of the shuddering bus, the watcher did not stir. Only his eyes continued their steady gaze, and the conductor felt excruciatingly tortured as they drilled the message of his guilt into his consciousness. Outrage alternated with a sweaty fear he had never before felt. Something, it seemed to him, was being drained from him, leaving the body feeling like a very dry sponge, very light, completely at the mercy of slight toying gusts of wind.

Then, very suddenly, the silence of the watcher filled him with an exhilarating kind of hope, and looking back into the

4

moment just lived through, the conductor wordlessly chided himself for the childishness of his fears. For, after all, how had he so frightened himself into thinking of the watcher as the bringer of his doom? Why had he placed the silent one above himself? Was it not likely, most probable, indeed, quite certain, that the watcher was himself also a man of skin and fat, with a stomach and a throat which needed to be served?

Calmly, the conductor slipped a hand into his shirt pocket and took out a packet of Embassy cigarettes. He had not thought he would have to open it so soon, but now there was a cause. The soul of a man was waiting to be drawn. An important bargain was hanging in the air. The conductor cleared his throat and ate the phlegm.

'Brother,' he said, inclining the prized cigarettes toward his desired accomplice, 'brother, you care for jot?' Still the staring eyes seemed to be holding for a better price. The conductor felt some of the first fear come back. He began walking as calmly as he could to the back of the bus.

'You see, we can share,' he said, as he came up to the man. But only the unending rattle of the bus answered and absorbed his words. The man in the back seat just sat and his eyes just stared, even when the conductor brought his cigarettes to within about a foot of his face. The giver's discomfort now gave place to keen curiosity, and he bent down to look into the staring face, a conciliating smile upon his own.

Then a savage indignation filled the conductor. For in the soft vibrating light inside the bus, he saw, running down from the left corner of the watcher's mouth, a stream of the man's spittle. Oozing freely, the oil-like liquid first entangled itself in the fingers of the watcher's left hand, underneath which it spread and touched the rusty metal lining of the seat with a dark sheen, then descended with quiet invitability down the dirty aged leather of the seat itself, losing itself at last in the depression made by the joint. The watcher was no watcher after all, only a sleeper.

Words shot out angrily from the conductor's mouth with an explosive imperiousness that woke the sleeper.

'You bloodyfucking sonofabitch! Article of no commercial value! You think the bus belongs to your grandfather?'

The sleeper awoke and looked up at his accuser, understanding nothing of the words at first. He licked the wetness around his chin, but the operation was unsuccessful. The mess was more than he had realized, and he had to wipe it off with his palm. He looked at his hand, all covered with his own viscous ooze. The conductor, now thoroughly furious, stood above him, sternly pointing to the seat in front.

'Are you a child? You vomit your smelly spit all over the place. Why? You don't have a bedroom?'

The man looked down on his glistening offense. Shame dwarfed him inside and he hastened to clean it. For some reason, perhaps out of sheer absence of mind, he thrust his right hand into his trouser pocket. When the hand emerged, it dragged after itself not a handkerchief, but the gray baft lining of the pocket, together with a small mess of old bus tickets. Apologetically the man stuffed the lining back into its hiding place and looked at the seat with his mouthwater on it. In a moment he made up his mind. Sitting deliberately on the seat, he leaned against the back leather and, moving his trunk sideways a few times, wiped the moisture off.

The conductor laughed a crackling laugh. 'So countryman, you don't have a handkerchief too.'

The man did not answer. He looked at the seat and saw that it was as dry as it could be under the circumstances. But the conductor's ridicule had turned to hostility again.

'Well,' he shouted above the death rattle of the bus, 'get out!'

The man had already started out of the bus, saying not a word. As he got to the bottom step, the conductor, sitting down on a seat next to one of the windows, looked out of the bus and shouted his farewell to him, 'Or were you waiting to shit in the bus?'

The man's foot hit the street and he moved slowly down the side past the front of the bus, peering ahead in the misty dawn air. The conductor's voice rolled out its message, enveloping the man with it. As he walked by the driver, the driver coughed, a short, violent cough which ended with a hoarse growl as he cleared his stuffed throat. Then he collected his full force and aimed the blob far out in front of him.

The man who had come out of the bus felt the accompanying spray settle on his cheek and on one side of his upper lip. He looked back in the anger of the moment, only to see the driver unrepentantly preparing his throat and mouth for one more effort. He quickened his pace somewhat.

The shimmering circles of dim light coming from the stationary bus, focused with oblique haziness on the side of the road, caught in their confusion what seemed to be a small pile of earth with a sort of signboard standing nonsensically on top of it. As the man got closer, the mound assumed a different shape and the signboard acquired the dimensions of a square waste box.

The thing had been a gleaming white sign when it was first installed, and that was not so very long ago. Now even the lettering on it was no longer decipherable. It was covered over thickly with the juice of every imaginable kind of waste matter. But once the letters had said in their brief brightness:

K.C.C. Receptacle For Disposal Of Waste

That was printed in blue. Underneath, in bolder capitals executed in lucent red, was the message:

Keep Your Country Clean
By Keeping Your City Clean

The box was one of the few relics of the latest campaign to rid the town of its filth. Like others before it, this campaign had been extremely impressive, and admiring rumors indicated that it had cost a great lot of money. Certainly the papers had been full of words informing their readers that dirt was undesirable and must be eliminated. On successive days a series of big shots had appealed to everybody to be clean. The radio had run a program featuring a doctor, a Presbyterian priest, and a senior lecturer brought down from the University of Legon. The three had seemed to be in agreement about the evil effects of

7

uncleanliness. People were impressed. Judging by the volume of words printed and spoken, it was indeed, as the Principal Secretary to the Ministry of Health stated at the durbar held to round it off, the most magnificent campaign yet.

It was at the durbar that the little boxes had been launched. In the words of the principal secretary, they would be placed at strategic points all over the city, and they would serve, not just as containers for waste matter, but as shining examples of cleanliness.

In the end not many of the boxes were put out, though there was a lot said about the large amount of money paid for them. The few provided, however, had not been ignored. People used them well, so that it took no time at all for them to get full. People still used them, and they overflowed with banana peels and mango seeds and thoroughly sucked-out oranges and the chaff of sugarcane and most of all the thick brown wrapping from a hundred balls of *kenkey*. People did not have to go up to the boxes any more. From a distance they aimed their rubbish at the growing heap, and a good amount of juicy offal hit the face and sides of the box before finding a final resting place upon the heap. As yet the box was still visible above it all, though the writing upon it could no longer be read.

As he passed by the box, the walker put his hand in his right trouser pocket and pulled out the debris of used tickets and threw everything on the heap. At the curve in the road he stopped a while, his gaze directed downward as if he was trying to make up his mind about something. When he began to cross over to the other side of the road, his eyes were still fixed on the tar in front of him, and he walked quite slowly.

Abruptly the headlights of a fast-advancing car caught him in their powerful brightness. In that hasty second the man was far too startled even to move. Instead, he raised his eyes in a puzzled, helpless gesture and got in them the full blinding force of the light. The scrape of braking tires on the hard road and the stench of burning rubber hit him, bringing him out of his long half-sleep. Just in front of him the car stood with its tires sharply arced toward the safe center of the road. It was a shiny new taxi, and it was still bobbing gently up and down from the

8

sudden halt. The man recovered from his numbness, and took the few remaining steps to the side of the road. There, away from the overpowering glare of the headlights, he saw the dim outline of the taxi driver's head as it thrust itself out through the window. For long moments of silent incredulousness the taxi driver stared at the man, doubtless looking him up and down several times. Then in a terrible calm voice he began, 'Uncircumcised baboon.' The taxi driver spoke as if the words he was uttering expressed only the most banal of truths. 'Moron of a frog. If your time has come, search for someone else to take your worthless life.'

The man took a step forward in order to be closer to the taxi driver, and said apologetically, 'I wasn't looking. I'm sorry.'

But the apology only seemed to inflame the taxi driver's temper. 'Sorry my foot,' he said with a cutting softness in his voice. 'Next time look where you're going.' He started his engine running again, and as the car began to ease itself forward, he exploded in a final access of uncontrollable ire, 'Your mother's rotten cunt!'

The engine's smooth sound rose evenly as the car gathered speed, gradually dying down as the distance absorbed the speeding vehicle.

The man moved a little less slowly now, keeping to the dark earth beside the gutter that ran the length of the road. He passed by the gloomy building of the Post Office, and his pace quickened involuntarily as he began descending the steep little hill beyond that. Across the road at the bottom the street lamps perfunctorily gave a certain illumination to the shapes of the row of old commercial buildings, and their light bounced dully off the corrugated iron shelters in front of the shop gates beneath which the watchmen slept. He passed by the U.T.C., the G.N.T.C., the U.A.C., and the French C.F.A.O. The shops had been there all the time, as far back as he could remember. The G.N.T.C., of course, was regarded as a new thing, but only the name had really changed with Independence. The shop had always been there, and in the old days it had belonged to a rich Greek and was known by his name, A. G. LEVENTIS. So in a way the thing was new. Yet the stories that were sometimes

9

heard about it were not stories of something young and vigorous, but the same old stories of money changing hands and throats getting moistened and palms getting greased. Only this time if the old stories aroused any anger, there was nowhere for it to go. The sons of the nation were now in charge, after all. How completely the new thing took after the old.

Behind the firms the dim mass of Yensua Hill rose from the ground. Where its form ended, it was now possible to see the sky, still dark but not so dark as the earth beneath. On top of the hill, commanding it just as it commanded the scene below, its sheer, flat, multistoried side an insulting white in the concentrated gleam of the hotel's spotlights, towered the useless structure of the Atlantic-Caprice. Sometimes it seemed as if the huge building had been put there for a purpose, like that of attracting to itself all the massive anger of a people in pain. But then, if there were any angry ones at all these days, they were most certainly feeling the loneliness of mourners at a festival of crazy joy. Perhaps then the purpose of this white thing was to draw onto itself the love of a people hungry for just something such as this. The gleam, in moments of honesty, had a power to produce a disturbing ambiguity within. It would be good to say that the gleam never did attract. It would be good, but it would be far from the truth. And something terrible was happening as time went on. It was getting harder to tell whether the gleam repelled more than it attracted, attracted more than it repelled, or just did both at once in one disgustingly confused feeling all the time these heavy days.

Down from the C.F.A.O., the food stands opposite the Block were all deserted, save for long orange rinds with their white insides strangely visible in the darkness, like some kind of fat worms lying around on the lip of the gutter before the road, and the less discernible corn husks that had held together now long-swallowed balls of *kenkey*. The man stopped uncertainly as he came to the large building opposite the stands. The Block. This was the Block.

The building never ceased to amaze with its squat massiveness. It did not seem possible that this thing could ever have been considered beautiful, and yet it seemed a great deal of

10

care had gone into the making of even the bricks of which it was made. Each brick had on it the huge imprint of something like a petal of the hibiscus flower slanted diagonally across it. Where the individual blocks met, a clear groove ran between them, so that from some angles the whole building looked like a pattern of vertical and horizontal lines. But this impression was to be had from certain chosen angles only. From most other points the picture made by the walls of the Block was much less pleasant. For years and years the building had been plastered at irregular intervals with paint and distemper, mostly of an official murk-yellow color. In the intervals, between successive layers of distemper, the walls were caressed and thoroughly smothered by brown dust blowing off the roadside together with swirling grit from the coal and gravel of the railroad yard within and behind, and the corners of walls where people passed always dripped with the engine grease left by thousands of transient hands. Every new coating, then, was received as just another inevitable accretion in a continuing story whose beginnings were now lost and whose end no one was likely to bother about. The spaces between the bricks were still there, but from most points they seemed about to get lost in a kind of waxen fusion. The flower patterns also had their crusts of paint, so that the whole thing gave a final impression of lumpy heaviness. Even in the daylight this impression persisted, and was in fact made deeper by the unnecessary boldness of the cement relief lettering out in front:

RAILWAY & HARBOUR ADMINISTRATION BLOCK
MCMXXVII

The man disappeared through the gigantic opening in the front of the building and turned up the broad cement stairs to the right. He moved absently to the left of the staircase and reached for the support of the banister, but immediately after contact his hand recoiled in an instinctive gesture of withdrawal. The touch of the banister on the balls of his fingertips had something uncomfortably organic about it. A weak bulb hung over the whole staircase suspended on some thin, invisible thread. By its light it was barely possible to see the

11

banister, and the sight was like that of a very long piece of diseased skin. The banister had originally been a wooden one, and to this time it was still possible to see, in the deepest of the cracks between the swellings of other matter, a dubious piece of deeply aged brown wood. And there were many cracks, though most of them did not reach all the way down to the wood underneath. They were no longer sharp, the cracks, but all rounded out and smoothed, consumed by some soft, gentle process of decay. In places the wood seemed to have been painted over, but that must have been long ago indeed. For a long time only polish, different kinds of wood and floor polish, had been used. It would be impossible to calculate how much polish on how many rags the wood on the stair banister had seen, but there was certainly enough Ronuk and Mansion splashed there to give the place its now indelible reek of putrid turpentine. What had been going on there and was going on now and would go on and on through all the years ahead was a species of war carried on in the silence of long ages, a struggle in which only the keen, uncanny eyes and ears of lunatic seers could detect the deceiving, easy breathing of the strugglers.

The wood underneath would win and win till the end of time. Of that there was no doubt possible, only the pain of hope perennially doomed to disappointment. It was so clear. Of course it was in the nature of the wood to rot with age. The polish, it was supposed, would catch the rot. But of course in the end it was the rot which imprisoned everything in its effortless embrace. It did not really have to fight. Being was enough. In the natural course of things it would always take the newness of the different kinds of polish and the vaunted cleansing power of the chemicals in them, and it would convert all to victorious filth, awaiting yet more polish again and again and again. And the wood was not alone.

Apart from the wood itself there were, of course, people themselves, just so many hands and fingers bringing help to the wood in its course toward putrefaction. Left-hand fingers in their careless journey from a hasty anus sliding all the way up the banister as their owners made the return trip from the lavatory downstairs to the offices above. Right-hand fingers still

12

dripping with the after-piss and the stale sweat from fat crotches. The calloused palms of messengers after they had blown their clogged noses reaching for a convenient place to leave the well-rubbed moisture. Afternoon hands not entirely licked clean of palm soup and remnants of *kenkey*. The wood would always win.

CHAPTER TWO

The dimness of the morning made all colors inside the office itself look very strange. The windows to the left and right now had an oily yellow shine which hid their underlying color. Near the center, where the day clerks' huge table stood, all the wooden chairs had been placed in two long rows, leaning forward against the long edges of the table.

As the man passed by the table his hand brushed against the backrest of one of the chairs and slid to the end joint. There were spots on the chair that had almost the same feel as the banister, and, without actually thinking of his movements at all, the man found himself rubbing his thumb against the finger that had touched the chair most closely, as if he expected to find some soft, moist piece of the chair or the banister sticking to it.

From the office floor the light came dully, like a ball whose bounce had died completely. In between the individual wooden tiles the accumulated dirt and polish had a color that seemed even in the dimness a little lighter than that of the wood. In a few places it actually stood up in thin ridges, causing the feet to drag just a little.

At the control desk the night clerk was still in his seat, but he had fallen asleep. His head was resting heavily on his right arm, which he had tried to bend into a comfortable pillow. The arm had slipped to one side, so that the clerk's head was now touching the top of the table in the crook of his arm. The other arm hung loose, now and then swinging almost imperceptibly by the exhausted clerk's chair.

The man walked noiselessly toward the sleeper and touched him very gently. At first there was no response, but the man kept a gentle pressure on the clerk's shoulder, increasing it till he woke up. The sleeper woke up in the grip of a brief, strong terror. As he came up from his easy darkness his face lost its

14

softness and became strained, like the face of a person who had just arrived at a decision to do something terribly painful but also very necessary. And his mouth was twisted, out of control.

'What? What?' the clerk asked, his voice uneasy, almost shouting.

The man looked levelly at the waking sleeper and smiled. The smile seemed to reassure the clerk, and the terror vanished from his face.

'Ah, contrey,' he said, 'I tire.' As he spoke he drew two fingers across his cheeks and mouth in a slow, pensive gesture.

'There was a lot of work last night?' the man asked.

'No, contrey,' said the other, 'not work. But when man is alone here all through the night . . .'

'I know,' said the man, also shaking his head.

'Oh, you don't know, contrey,' the clerk continued as if he had not heard. 'You don't know how last night was bad for me.'

'What happened?'

For a long while the clerk gave no answer, only staring at the man as if something about him aroused a huge amount of suspicion. Then, with a suddenness that amazed the listening man, he said, 'Nothing. Nothing, contrey, nothing. But I sat here alone, and I was wishing somebody would come in, and all night long there was nobody. Me alone.'

This was very true of the night shift. Very true of the dead nights when whole long hours could go by pierced only by the departing sounds of goods trains, lone and empty. On certain nights – these last days they were not only Saturday nights, but other nights as well – the loneliness was made a bit more bitter by the distant beat of bands on the hill creating happiness for those able to pay money at all times of the month, to pay money and to get change for it – the men of the Atlantic-Caprice. Sometimes also the sudden blast of car horns coming briefly and getting swallowed again forever, each particular sound going somewhere very far away. And underneath these single cries the night itself, a long, unending sound within the

15

ear, just too high or just too low to disturb the captive hearer. Then the mocking rattle of the Morse machine mercifully breaking now and then into the frightening sameness of the lonely time.

'Once,' the clerk said, 'I wanted to stop and get out. About two in the morning.'

'Where did you go?'

'I didn't go. When I thought of it, where could I go?'

'Home,' the man said, laughing a little.

'Home?' The other made a sound much like dry paper tearing. Was it meant as an answering laugh? 'I thought of home.' The brightness in his eyes went down and the eyeballs themselves seemed to retreat inside, getting darker. He paused, unable to make up his mind about something, then he added, 'I can almost like it here when I think of home.'

The man laughed a much softer laugh and let his silence swallow up the words. 'Anyway,' he said finally, 'nothing went wrong?'

'No,' the clerk said. 'At Kojokrom the control telephone is dead again.'

'As usual.'

'Yes, as usual.'

'And the others?'

'Some trouble with most of the lines,' said the night clerk. 'Benso was all right at first, but went dead from time to time. Esuaso too.'

The man sighed. 'Always the same old things not working.'

'You can use the Morse,' said the clerk. 'Nothing wrong with that.'

'Fine,' said the man.

'I haven't finished logging everything yet,' the clerk said. 'I'm going to do it now.'

He turned again, took out a pen stuck between the center pages of the thick logbook, and began to write.

The man looked at the control graph above the big desk. The lines were not too many, and only two of them were red. Passenger trains. One of these red lines went evenly from the bottom

16

terminus, Kansawora, all the way up to Kumasi with only a couple of brief stops. The other red line came down just as evenly, making the same number of brief stops. Express trains.

The rest were goods and manganese trains. The night clerk had chosen to mark the goods trains with green, not lead, and this had made the pattern very clear and quite beautiful just to look at. The goods and manganese trains had sometimes had to wait long periods for other trains to pass. In places they had been shunted aside for the express trains to pass, but there were other places where they seemed to have stopped for nothing at all.

The night clerk took a long time completing the log. When at last he had finished, he closed the book and got up off the center chair.

As the night clerk said good-bye and walked out, the man moved over to the center chair facing the graph. From the drawer to his left he took out a whole handful of pencils, then got up and walked over to the pencil sharpener fixed to the table at its right end. When he stuck a pencil into the sharpener and turned the handle, the handle sped round and round with the futile freedom of a thing connected to nothing else. The man stopped trying and went back to his seat. Searching deep inside the drawer, he found an old blade. He began to sharpen the pencils at the same time reading over the night clerk's log, just checking.

The night clerk had not written the date, but everything else was carefully written down in a neat hand:

On duty, 10 P.M. – 6 A.M.
Control telephones: Faulty at Kojokrom
Benso
Esuaso
Carrier faulty.
Other stations in good operating order.
Manganese:
Four trains tonight.
No trains tomorrow.

Goods trains canceled
39G   No power.
29G   No guard (due accident en route).
Allocation of tracks:
Rail car leaving Kansawora Station tomorrow for Esuaso.
Occupant, Section Engineer. Leaves 08.00 A.M.
Accident: Class B, between Benso and Esuaso.

J. K. Ackonu.
Night Control Clerk.

The man added his own signature to that of the night clerk and opened the logbook at a fresh page.

Just then the door opened and the first messenger entered, smiling.

'Hello controller,' he said cheerfully.

'Hello.'

The control telephone rang. 'Control, Kansawora,' the man said into the mouthpiece.

'Ah, you're there,' said the voice at the other end. 'Stationmaster, Angu, here.'

'Yes.'

'15G arrived Angu 6:02 A.M. Out 6:11. Book time.'

'Fine.' The man put the receiver down.

The messenger came over to the control desk. He still had his smile.

'You look happy,' the man said to him.

The messenger continued to smile, in the embarrassed way of a young girl confessing love. 'I won something in the lottery,' he said.

'Lucky you,' the man said. 'How much?'

The messenger hesitated before replying. 'One hundred cedis.'

'That's not very much,' the man laughed.

'I know,' said the messenger. 'But so many people would jump on me to help me eat it.'

'They'll come, anyway.'

'No. Nobody will know.'

'You used a nickname?'

18

'Help Me Oh God.' He smiled.

'I hope you have a nice time,' the man said.

The messenger frowned. 'I am happy, but I'm afraid,' he said.

'Juju?' the man smiled.

'No, not that,' said the messenger. 'But you know our Ghana.'

'Ah yes.'

'And everybody says the Ghana lottery is more Ghanaian than Ghana.'

'You're afraid you won't get your money?'

'I know people who won more than five hundred cedis last year. They still haven't got their money.'

'Have they been to the police?'

'For what?'

'To help them get their money.'

'You're joking,' said the messenger with some bitterness.

'It costs you more money if you go to the police, that's all.'

'What will you do?' the man asked.

'I hope some official at the lottery place will take some of my hundred cedis as a bribe and allow me to have the rest.' The messenger's smile was dead.

'You will be corrupting a public officer.' The man smiled.

'This is Ghana,' the messenger said, turning to go. The Morse machine sprang to life.

'Kojokrom Station.'

'Kansawora here.'

'Checking. What time Ch. Eng. Coming?'

'Leaves Kansawora 08:00 A.M.

'Thanks.'

'Righto.'

After eight the office began filling up rapidly as the day clerks came in with their little jokes and the talk of brief pay days and perennial Passion Weeks. Then the work of the day ended the talk, and even those who had little to do were reduced to silence because the rising heat was itself a very tiring thing.

CHAPTER THREE

After twelve even those within could tell the sun had risen very high. The rusty painted fan above was turned on, but it travelled with such tired slowness that it made more noise than air and made the Traffic Control Office uncomfortable in a strange indeterminate way. It was not the heat alone or the inside wetness alone. And it was not the useless sounds of the fan mixing with the usual rattle of the little Morse machines. It was the combination that created the sense of confusion which it would be impossible to fix and against which it would be merely foolish to protest. The wetness within came partly from the sea which was only a little way away. Sometimes it was possible to taste very clearly the salt that had been eating the walls and the paint on them, if one cared to run one's hand down the dripping surfaces and taste the sticky mess. Partly, too, the wetness came from people, everybody who worked in the office. Everybody seemed to sweat a lot, not from the exertion of their jobs, but from some kind of inner struggle that was always going on. So the sea salt and the sweat together and the fan above made this stewy atmosphere in which the suffering sleepers came and worked and went dumbly back afterward to homes they had earlier fled. There was really no doubt that it was like that in all their homes, everywhere save for those who had found in themselves the hardness for the upward climb. And he was not one of those.

At half past twelve the lines had cleared as usual. Only a few goods trains would be coming down, and there was nothing going up with which they could possibly collide. It was the time for sending self-pitying jokes along the Morse wire to the railwaymen shunted onto some dead siding where they could get rich in gift livestock and crops and eat their hearts out with the suicidal desire to get back to the warm center. Until the old 1:50 train started up to bring Tarkwa gold and Aboso manganese to the waiting Greek ships in the harbor, this would be the time of peace.

The man sent a message to whoever was in the Insu Siding office now. 'Handing over till two.'

A friendly rattle answered him. At first it was meaningless, just a good musical rhythm. When it resolved itself, it said, 'Yes lunchtime.'

Without thinking of what he was saying, the man tapped out, 'No food.'

Insu Siding answered, 'Plenty here.'

And a conversation had begun.

'Lucky.'

'Come. Transfer. Easy.'

'Can't.'

'Why?'

'Secret.'

'Family?'

'Secret.'

The rattle came again from Insu Siding, this time not so irreverent, not so joyful and musical, but a soft, sympathetic signing off, as if the other one were trying to say he did not know but he could understand. The man answered with a short rattle, looked at the machine with a wondering thought about how close people sometimes come to opening up their sores for others to see, and then he called to the man at the machine on his left. 'Over to you.'

The reply, as usual, came automatically, 'All correct.'

He moved slowly downstairs, past the banister and the light bulb under all the cobwebs. At the bottom, when he reached the entrance, he went out into the street with the sun shining all over it and the dust rising with the heat waves on it. He did it more out of habit than anything else, and before he got close enough to pick the words out of the noise of the sellers and the buyers of food, he turned left and walked down the right side of the road, down toward the harbor.

At a time like this, when the month was so far gone and all there was was the half-life of Passion Week, lunchtime was not a time to refresh oneself. Unless, of course, one chose to join the increasing numbers who had decided they were so deep in despair that there was nothing worse to fear in life. These were the men who had finally, and so early, so surprisingly early, seen enough of something in their own lives and in the lives around them to convince them of the final futility of efforts to break the mean monthly cycle of debt and borrowing, borrowing and debt. Nothing was left beyond the necessity of digging oneself deeper and deeper into holes in which there could never be anything like life. But perhaps the living dead could take some solace in the half-thought that there were so many others dead in life with them. So many, so frighteningly many, that maybe in the end even the efforts one made not to join them resulted only in another, more frustrating kind of living death.

Thinking of the endless round that shrinks a man to something less than the size and the meaning of little short-lived flying ants on rainy nights, the man followed the line of the hard steel tracks where they curved out and away from inside the loco yard and straightened out ahead for the melancholy piercing push into the interior of the land. On the gravel bed beneath the metal the mixture of fallen ashes and stray lumps of engine coal and steamed grease raised somewhere in the region of his throat the overwarm stench of despair and the defeat of a domestic kitchen well used, its whole atmosphere made up of malingering tongues of the humiliating smoke of all those yesterdays. Out ahead, however, the tracks drove straight in clean shiny lines and the air above the steel shook with the power of the sun until all the afternoon things seen through the air seemed fluid and not solid anymore. The sourness that had been gathering in his mouth went imperceptibly away until quite suddenly all he was aware of was the exceedingly sharp clarity of vision and the clean taste that comes with the successful defiance of hunger. It was not painful watching the little scratched-out farms of Northern migrant workers slide slowly past. Only a little effort, scarcely noticeable, was required to keep the footsteps landing on the warm crossties. In the ditch running along the left track, the unconquerable filth was beginning to cake together in places, though underneath it all

22

some water still managed to flow along. Nothing oppressed him as he walked along now, and even the slight giddiness accompanying the clarity of his starved vision was buried way beneath the unaccustomed happy lightness.

Some way out, the tracks went over a small ridge of concrete and cement, and the mud sliming alongside dipped underneath. The man crossed the bridge, then turned at the end and sat on the flanking cement embankment on the right. The bridge itself must have been built solidly enough, but the embankments must have been something in the nature of an afterthought. Where he sat on the right, a hunk of heavy cement had parted from the whole and fallen leaning into the thick stream coming out from under the bridge and formed a kind of dam. Behind it, all the filth seemed to have got caught for a hanging moment, so that the water escaping through a gap made by the little dam and the far side of the ditch had a cleanness which had nothing to do with the thing it came out from. Even from the small height of the dam, the water hit the bottom of the ditch with sufficient force to eat away the soft soil down to the harder stuff beneath, exposing a bottom of smooth sandy pebbles with the clear water now flowing over it. How long-lasting the clearness? Far out, toward the mouth of the small stream and the sea, he could see the water already aging into the mud of its beginnings. He drew back his gaze and was satisfied with the clearness of a quiet attraction, not at all like the ambiguous disturbing tumult within awakened by the gleam. And yet here undoubtedly was something close enough to the gleam, this clearness, this beautiful freedom from dirt. Somehow, there seemed to be a purity and a peace here which the gleam could never bring.

From the direction of the yard the wailing whistle of an old steam engine came down the lines and disappeared with its disturbing slowness into the shimmering distance behind him. The sound brought with it a vague taste of sorrow which rapidly grew until the man was asking himself questions that were no longer new to him but to which he had no hope of finding any answer, so insubstantial was the thing they strained to grasp. Why, between here and there, was it necessary that there should be a connection? Why was it that just the solitary whistle of a train about to disappear down the deep distances of the forest should scatter in the air so much of the feeling of permanent sorrow? To the clarity of his famished vision had been added a sharp sadness as he rose ready to return. The dryness in his nostrils persisted, and there was no moisture either in his mouth or in his eyes. The thought of food now brought with it a picture of its eating and its spewing out, of its beginnings and endings, so that no desire arose asking to be controlled. He walked quietly back the way he had come, looking at all the things he had seen on his way outward with the same clear vision, walking steadily back along the lines, into the dusty road and past the remnants of the groups of workers out for the afternoon break, and it was not until he went in and began again the climb up into the Control Office that the darkness of the place itself misted over the sharpness of everything he saw.

With the climb up into the office, thoughts that might have struck desperation into him on other days came with a surprising gentleness. The grown man eats his guts, so, having started, he might as well make the killing effort now and relax afterward, if that would be possible. So when he opened the door into the Control Office he did not go directly to his own place at the long table with the line diagrams up in front of it; he went instead past the table to the end of the office and stood waiting in front of the counter there while the small man behind it read and reread with a crucified frown the day's four little frames of 'Garth.' Showing no signs of having finally fathomed the mystery of the strip, the little man just gave up and blinked up at the waiting man. His nostrils every few seconds accomplished an involuntary sideways twitch which made his attempts to adopt an air of importance not just ridiculous but actually irritating in the special way in which the efforts of a Ghanaian struggling to talk like some Englishman are irritating.

'Erm, wort cin I dew for yew?' Frantic, rapid, singsong delivery, air of self-congratulation after a brilliant speech, twitching nose, the blind fool.

'Slip.' Idiot's face a mask of puzzlement; what on earth is there to feel puzzled about?

'Eouvatime sleps, yew mean?' As if any other slips could have been meant. Strain of the accent produces a double twitch this time; after this the whole face collapses in an equally involuntary spell of relaxation.

'Yes, overtime slips.'

Now the little man produces a smile of intimate familiarity. From a drawer to his right he brings out the pad of slips. 'Is a joke,' he says. The man is thankful that his accent is now relaxed and natural, but he gives no answer. As he fills out the slip and signs it, the little man volunteers, 'Money swine!' Still no answer. The little man retreats into his official position. 'Seouw. Nine eouclock.'

'Seven o'clock.'

The little man squints dramatically at the slip. 'Eouw. Yes, 7 P.M. I see, I see.'

The man watched silently as the little man put the slip in with the others, then he turned and walked back to his seat at the long control table. The man at his left did not have to say anything. Nothing much had happened.

He sat down facing the huge chart with all the lines and the millipede names of slow stations alongside them. Nothing much had happened. Nothing much would happen. The traffic of the afternoon was as usual very slow and very sparse. Perhaps from some side station near a mine, a quiet line of open wagons with cracked boards held together with rusty plates and rivets would slide along the hot rails to a languid stop some forgotten place, to wait for other slow days when it would get shunted back and down to the sea far away. After a while it was possible not to be aware of the noises of the fan. On the Morse machine there was a long roll that could only raise thoughts of people going irretrievably crazy at the long end of the telegraph. Maybe also the famous rattle of men preparing to die. In a while, when it was no longer possible to ignore the rattle, the man tapped back once for silence, then tapped out the message, 'Shut up.'

The roll came again, defiantly insistent. The maniac at the

25

end of the line had grown indignant. Another rap. Short silence. Then the man asks in half-conciliation, 'Who be you?'

A roll now, very long and very senseless. But at the very end it carries a signature, 'Obuasi.'

That at least was something, and should deserve a reply.

The man held the Morse knob again, lightly. 'Hello.'

With amazing speed an answer comes back, this time entirely coherent, decipherable at the last. 'Why do we agree to go on like this?' Then again the rattle.

The question was repeated several times, alternating with long unanswered rolls on the machine. To stop himself from cutting off the sound in anger the man turned and just watched the fan, only just then another feeble, useless movement would happen and the blades would be drawn through another arc. Only a long hour later did the noise finally stop – 4:30 P.M.

With a hurry that was still instinctive after so many years of disappointment and so much knowledge of futility, the clerks put away the things they called work and make for the door. What did they think they were hurrying to? But perhaps it must be said that at the moment they did not really care about having nothing worth rushing to. All they knew was that they were fleeing.

'Good night.'

'Good night.'

'Bye-bye-o.'

'Bye-o.'

It was a terrible truth but the oppressiveness of the office was not so heavy with the others gone. It was there still, but there were not all those faces and thick bodies confirming it, and it was easier to think of it, to have the mind get hold of it as if it could someday be conquered. The world was once again not here, not present with its terrible closeness, but something outside. Why was it such a strong and ancient thought, that there was nothing in loneliness but pain?

The Morse rattled off quiet details of coming trains, and a message came down the telephone line all the way from Konongo.

'Ferguson, 5:21 mine train nine minutes late to Kansawora.'

'Present position, please?'

'Nsuta B, approaching A.'

'Thank you.'

'Thank you.'

The comforting loneliness again. The man moved the little green way flags down the lines on the big wall chart.

'Ferguson, 5:21 thirteen minutes late.'

'. . . minutes late.'

In through the door came a belly swathed in *kente* cloth. The feet beneath the belly dragged themselves and the mass above in little arcs, getting caught in angular ends of heavy cloth. Sandals made of thick leather, encrusted with too many tufts and useless knobs, but then the wearer's pride had something to do with tassels. The visitor looked around and saw no one except the man.

'Good even,' the visitor shouted, moving forward.

'Evening.'

The visitor's mouth was a wolf shape and when he spoke the reason appeared. Children had a name for such teeth. Nephews, they called these teeth which come in rows, a second and even a third set pushing impatiently out against the first. The man reached over to his right and switched on the light immediately above himself and turned squarely to face the visitor.

'I am looking for the allocation clerk,' the visitor said. His wolf mouth was agape in a gesture that must have been meant for a smile, a thing that was totally unnecessary and irritating.

'Which one?'

'Which one?' In his puzzlement the visitor made an involuntary movement to close his snout. But the lip flesh, though abundant, proved insufficient and hung around the generations of teeth, vainly straining to meet over them.

'There are two clerks. One for time, one for wagon space.'

'Aha, I understand now.' The visitor smiled again. 'Wagons. It's wagons I have come to talk about.'

'Space allocation. You should come earlier in the day, though. In this office the clerks go home at four-thirty.'

'Oh, I know,' the teeth said. 'I know, but I thought he would stay after work.'

'Had you fixed a time with him?'

'Actually, no. But someone told me this was about the right time to come.'

'To come for what?' the man asked.

The flesh of the snout accomplished a grotesque retreat from the teeth, and the visitor hesitated, thinking of a way to put what he was about to say.

'Actually,' he said at last, 'actually, it is a bit private.' His eyes ranged over the chart behind the man. He gathered up the folds of his *kente* cloth in the angle of his right arm and flung the whole collected heap onto his shoulder. His lips worked forward and back a couple of times over his tortured gums. Then he seemed to make up his mind about the thing that was making him so restless.

'Brother,' the many teeth said, 'brother, you also can help me.'

'Me?' The man had not expected this.

'Yes, brother,' the visitor said. 'And I will make you know that you have really helped me.' The lips had this habit of leaving in their wake bubbles and lines of filmy saliva whose yellow color was not all from the bulb above.

'I am not the booking clerk,' the man said. 'The booking clerk has gone home.'

'I know, brother, I know.' The visitor no longer looked past the man at the chart behind him on the wall. Now he was looking almost directly into his eyes. On his face was a strained expression produced by his desire to penetrate the man's incomprehension, partly by the structure of the face itself.

'He will be in tomorrow morning.'

The visitor cleared his throat in exasperation. 'Brother,' he asked, 'why are you making everything so difficult for me?'

The outburst took the man completely by surprise, so that what he said next came entirely by itself. 'Now what have I done?' The man saw the visitor draw closer.

'I should be asking you that question,' the visitor said. 'I should be asking you people in this office what have I done to you. Why do you treat me this way?' The man just stared, and was lost completely in his surprise at the visitor's words and his fascination with his teeth. Listening to the words required a real effort now. 'You know me,' the teeth said aggressively. 'You know my name.'

'I don't know your name,' the man said quietly. The visitor looked as if he had been getting ready to say something or other, but had been struck dumb by incredulity. He looked at the man with eyes that were now too steady and smiled a smile that had in it the tolerant sourness of unbelief.

'Amankwa,' the visitor said at last. 'They call me Amankwa. I cut timber. Contractor.'

'If you can come back tomorrow . . .' the man was saying. But now the sick conciliatory smile had receded from the visitor's face and in its place there was the impotent resentment of a cheated man.

'My friend,' he said, 'all joke aside. Come with me inside the forest and I will show you something to make you weep. Do you know, I cut my timber a long time ago and it is still waiting in the forest. Half of it will be rotten soon. Why do you have to treat me like that? What do you want?'

'I am sorry,' the man answered, 'but I have nothing to do with allocations.'

'I am not a child, my friend. If you work in the same office you can eat from the same bowl. What do you mean to tell me?'

'I have my job; the booking clerk has his job. I don't interfere with him.'

'Why not? Why not?' The visitor spoke with open heat. 'You think my timber should rot in the forest? Look, they tell me all the time, no wagons, no space. But many times I see wagons coming down here, carrying nothing but stones. Sometimes empty, my good friend, empty. Is that how to do it?'

'If you want to talk to someone higher up . . .'

'My friend,' the visitor said, 'don't joke with me. I need to talk to you.'

'I tell you I have nothing to do with bookings.'

'You can see that clerk for me.' The visitor looked suspiciously toward the door, then plunged his left arm underneath his *kente* folds. When the arm emerged it was clutching a dark brown leather wallet. The wallet was not fat. The man looked steadily at the visitor. The visitor's gaze was bent, his eyes looking in the wallet while thick fingers fumbled inside. Then the fingers brought out two carefully held-out notes, two green tens. The man said nothing. The visitor put the ten-cedi notes under a stone paperweight on the table behind the man, to his right. The visitor drew his hand back from the table and the notes and stood staring at the man in front of him. The man said nothing.

'Take it,' the visitor said. 'One for you, one for him.'

'Why should I?'

The look on the visitor's face made it plain that to this kind of question no sane man would give an answer. But then suddenly the visitor's expression changed, and he laughed a laugh that came out too high, like a woman's or a child's.

'You are a funny man, you this man,' he said. 'You think I am a fool to be giving you just ten cedis?' Again the high laugh. 'Is nothing. I know ten is nothing. So, my friend, what do you drink?'

The man looked levelly at the visitor and gave his answer. 'Water.'

This time the visitor bent double and his laugh was wild and forced and he took a few short steps across the floor holding his belly as if it were about to burst with the pressure of his laughter. Then abruptly he straightened up and stopped in front of the man with a solemn look on his face, and the look had something of pain in it.

'I beg you, let us stop joking now,' the visitor said. 'They are waiting for me and I must go. A man is a man. I tell you what I will do. Take that one for yourself and give the other one to your friend. I myself will find some fine drink for you. Take it. Take it, my friend.'

The man looked at the face before him, pleading with the words of millions and the voice of ages, and he felt lonely in the way only a man condemned by all things around him can ever feel lonely. 'I will not take it,' he said, too quietly, perhaps.

The visitor did not touch his money. He did not even look at it. He only said, 'Look, I mean it. I offer you three times. Is good money.'

'I know.'

'Then take it.'

'No.' The man shook his head very gently, but there was a finality in the gesture which even the visitor could no longer mistake.

'You refuse?'

'Yes.'

The frown on the visitor's face made it impossible to judge whether the grimace was one of contempt or of self-pity. His hand touched the money lying on the table and stopped there.

'But why?' he shouted, 'why do you treat me so? What have I done against you? Tell me, what have I done?'

There was nothing the man could say now. He watched silently as the visitor took the two notes and slipped them back into the dark wallet.

'But what is wrong?' the visitor asked again.

'Wrong?'

'Yes my friend. Why do you behave like that?'

'I don't know,' the man said.

'I say my timber is rotting in the forest. You don't believe me.'

'I think I believe you.'

'Then what is this?' The visitor was angry now, in the special way the upright have of being angry with perverse people. He searched around under his folds of *kente* cloth and stuck the wallet in some hidden pocket. Then, saying not a word of farewell to the man at the table, he strode to the door, opened it angrily and disappeared behind it. The man was left alone with thoughts of the easy slide and how everything said there was something miserable, something unspeakably dishonest about a man who refused to take and to give what everyone around was busy taking and giving: something unnatural, something very cruel, something that was criminal, for who but a criminal could ever be left with such a feeling of loneliness?

He heard the door open again but did not look up. Around this time the night sweeper would come and do his work. Then a hand came to rest confidentially on his left shoulder, and he became aware of the rich must of *kente* cloth. He turned.

'You are not angry with me?' Once more the visitor's sick smile.

'Should I be?'

'No.' The visitor laughed low and relaxedly now. 'Tomorrow, what will you say to the other man?'

'Nothing.'

'Please don't be annoyed.' *Kente* folds slipping down, being pushed up over shoulder again. 'You see, I don't want to do anything bad. But I want to know what he wants. Only what he wants. I can give him what he wants.'

'To make a booking, you have to come during working hours.'

'All right, all right,' the visitor said. 'But you also know that everybody prospers from the work he does, no? Everybody prospers from the job he does.'

'Tomorrow morning.'

'So you won't say anything? Don't be annoyed. I was not tricking you.'

The door opened and the visitor turned sharply to look at the intruder. But the door just stayed open and no one seemed about to enter the office. The visitor could not take his eyes off the door. A bent bucket swung through the open door, and behind it came a small man lugging a brush and a mop with a handle taller than himself.

'Who is that?' The visitor asked that question before he could catch himself, and the man smiled at it.

'The sweeper. He cleans this place.'

The visitor looked with hostility at the newcomer and cleared his throat. 'I must go now,' he said. 'They are waiting for me.' He walked past the sweeper and went out.

The sweeper dragged his goods across the floor. His walk

32

was slow and dazed, and he was tired at the beginning of his night. The night was the end of a long day filled with two jobs pieced together, and the night cleaning job was number three. So even at the beginning of the night the sweeper was tired and almost walking in his sleep.

'Good evening, sah,' said this sleepwalker with a smile straight from the dead.

'Good evening, Atia.'

But the sleepwalker sweeper already had his head bent down and was beginning to drag his brush on the long walk from corner to corner, and he did not hear the answering greeting. No matter. A lost man from distances far off caught in a strange dance on the lower stair. Someone so much worse off. Christ! Someone actually worse off.

After a while the soggy sound of the wet mop replaced the soft drag of the brush and the sudden knocks as it hit the corners. Behind, the fan continued its languid turning and the light began again to weaken into an orange yellow color and then swell into whiteness in long, slow waves of time. A few minutes before seven the night relief came in. He was a new man just out of Secondary, very young, and he was whistling in his cheerful mood this terrible night. No doubt, being only new, he was calculating in his undisappointed mind that he would stay here only a short while and like a free man fly off to something closer to his soul. What in his breeziness he had yet to know was this: that his dream was not his alone, that everyone before him had crawled with hope along the same unending path, dreaming of future days when they would crawl no longer but run if they wanted to run, and fly if the spirit moved them. But along the streets, those who can soon learn to recognize in ordinary faces beings whom the spirit has moved, but who cannot follow where it beckons, so heavy are the small ordinary days of the time. The unwary freedom of the young man and the realization that it was time to go filled the man with an undefined fear of things that had not yet come. The young man greeted him happily.

'Evening,' the man replied. He got off the chair. 'You know what to do, of course. Use the telephone.'

'Okay.'

'Nothing much tonight. Slack time all along the line. The night trains are listed.' The man began to walk toward the door.

'Good night,' the young man shouted after him.

'Good night.'

At the door the sleepwalker was also about to leave. He put his load down and held the door open for the man, smiling again and giving a final greeting. The man began to descend the stairs. In his tiredness it did not matter that his thumb and the balls of his fingertips were being clammily caressed by the caked accretions on the banister. As he went down a shadow rose up the bottom wall to meet him, and it was his own.

CHAPTER FOUR

Outside, the sight of the street itself raised thoughts of the re-proach of loved ones, coming in silent sounds that ate into the mind in wiry spirals and stayed there circling in tightening rings, never letting go. There was no hurry. At the other end there was only home, the land of the loved ones, and there it was only the heroes of the gleam who did not feel that they were strangers. And he had not the kind of hardness that the gleam required. Walking with the slowness of those whose desire has nowhere to go, the man moved up the road, past the lines of evening people under the waning lamps selling green and yellow oranges and bloated bread polished with leftover oil, and little tins and packets of things no one was in any hurry to buy. Under a dying lamp a child is disturbed by a long cough coming from somewhere deep in the center of the infant body. At the end of it his mother calmly puts her mouth to the wet congested nostrils and sucks them free. The mess she lets fall gently by the roadside and with her bare foot she rubs it softly into the earth. Up at the top a bus arrives and makes the turn for the journey back. The man does not hurry. Let it go. From the other side of the road there is the indiscreet hiss of a night-walker also suffering through her Passion Week. At other times the hiss is meant only for the heroes, but now it comes clearly over. In the space between weak lamps opposite can be seen the fragile shine of some ornament on her. There are many of the walking dead, many so much worse off. The shine disappears then comes again, closer, somewhere near the middle of the road. Incredible. In a moment the air is filled with the sharp sweetness of arm-pit powder hot and moist, and the keenness of perfume trapped in creases of prematurely tired skin. At rapid intervals comes the vapor of a well-used wig. Horse or human? Alive or dead? And how long departed?

'Ssssssss.' The appeal is not directed anywhere beyond the

35

man. The incredible comes true at times like this. The man looks up and sees beneath the mass of the wig the bright circle of an earring. The walker does not see, or chooses not to see, the lukewarm apologetic smile.

'Five.' The voice is not a used one. It is almost like a shy child's. The man shakes his head. How anyhow at a time like this?

'Three.' Abrupt drop, this. So many desperate needs.

'Sister, I have nothing at all.' No response. Light glinting on swirled earring. The walker steps back into the ambiguous shadow between the lights, waiting with a strange voice for strange faces in the dark. More sellers under more faint lights, selling more of the same inconsequential things. From the rise ahead an object of power and darkness and gleaming light comes shimmering down in a potent moving stream, and it stops in front of a half-asleep seller close to the man. Above the cool murmur of the engine the voice of a female rises from within, thin as long wire stabbing into open eyes.

'Driver get some oranges.'

'How much, Auntie?'

'Oh, two dozen.'

The driver steps out and swings the door shut with the satisfied thud of newness. The wire voice within seems to wail something more, and from the back seat of the limousine a man dressed in a black suit comes out and makes straight for a little covered box with bread in it. The young girl behind the box hurries to open it and to hold out a large wrapped loaf. The man takes it and says, 'One more.'

The girl pulls out another. Glint of a fifty-pesewa coin. The man turns and walks confidently back to the car. The girl runs after him with his change, but he does not want it and the girl returns to her box. Next to the girl another, older seller wakes to her missed chance and begins to call out, 'Big man, I have fine bread.'

'I have bought some already.' The voice of the suited man had something unexpected about it, like a fisherman's voice with the sand and the salt hoarsening it forcing itself into unac-

36

customed English rhythms. Why was this necessary? A very Ghanaian voice.

'My lord,' comes the woman again, 'my big lord, this bread is real bread.'

Inside the big car the pointed female voice springs and coils around, complaining of fridges too full to contain anything more and of too much bread already bought. Outside, the seller sweetens her tones.

'My own lord, my master, oh, my white man, come. Come and take my bread. It is all yours, my white man, all yours.'

The car door opens and the suited man emerges and strides slowly toward the praise-singing seller. The sharp voice inside the car makes one more sound of impatience, then subsides, waiting. The suit stops in front of the seller, and the voice that comes out of it is playful, patronizing.

'Mammy, I can't eat all of that.'

'So buy for your wife,' the seller sings back.

'She has enough.'

'Your girl friends. Young, beautiful girls, no?'

'I have no girl friends.'

'Ho, my white man, don't make me laugh. Have you ever seen a big man without girls? Even the old ones,' the seller laughs, 'even the old men.'

'Mammy, I am different.' The suited man pays the seller. She takes the money and holds on to the man's hand, looking intently into his face now.

'You are a politician,' she says at last, 'a big man.'

'Who told you?'

'It's true is it not?' she asks. 'I have seen your picture somewhere.'

'I see.' The suited man looks around him. Even in the faint light his smile is easy to see. It forms a strange pattern of pale light with the material of his shirt, which in the space between the darkness of his suit seems designed to point down somewhere between the invisible thighs.

'Hell-low,' says the smile to the invisible man of the shadows, 'what are you doing here? I almost didn't see you.'

'Going home from work. At first I wasn't sure.'

A pale cuff flashes, and the suited man looks at his watch and just murmurs something to himself, very low. 'By the way,' he says, 'we'll be over to see you soon, Estie and myself.'

'Hmmm.'

'No. This time I mean it. Let's see. Today is Wednesday. Let's make it Satur . . . no, Sunday evening.'

'What time?'

'Nine I'll be free, I think.'

The car horn splits the air with its new, irritated sound, and the suited man spins instinctively around, then recovers and says, 'Estie is in the car. Come and greet her.'

The man walks behind the suit up to the car. The voice within starts, scolding in an abrasive tone, but the suit cuts it short. 'Estie, I found a stranger.'

The woman's wire voice changes a little in tone. 'Aaaa, ei look. I didn't see anybody.' Out through the window she holds out a hand and something glitters in the night light. The man takes the hand. Moist like lubricated flesh. It is withdrawn as quickly as if contact were a well-known calamity, and the woman inside seems plainly to have forgotten about the man outside. Another sound of a door softly closing. 'Well, Sunday, then. Nine.'

'Fine.'

A voice from the car, an afterthought as the engine turns impatiently. 'Oh, by the way, we are not going back. Atlantic-Caprice, and we are late. Otherwise . . .'

'Don't worry your soul,' the man hollers after the fluid movement of the limousine. 'Don't worry your soul . . .' he repeats the words in a whisper to himself, and turns his look away from the gleam above the hill.

The waiting period is a time of comforting emptiness. thoughts that do not necessarily have to have anything to do with the sickness of despair come and go leaving nothing painful behind them. How many hands passing over the long bar of the bench at the bus stop since it was first put there? What do three lit windows mean in the dark Post Office at night? What have the others waiting been doing? With a wholly unnecessary burst of noise a bus comes and stops with its entrance door a

38

yard beyond the bus stop opening. The waiting people slide toward it, but the conductor walks away down the road. In a few moments the waiters can hear the sound of his urine hitting the clean-your-city can. He must be aiming high. Everyone relaxes visibly. The poor are rich in patience. The driver in his turn jumps down and follows the conductor to the heap. His sound is much more feeble. For a long time they stand by the heap laughing and talking. Joking about what has just been going on? Comparing what? The driver wanders back, climbs in and goes to sleep over the wheel. The conductor is aiming to go down in the direction of the sellers. A few, fed up with waiting, climb in anyhow and put their heads to rest against the remaining panes. Someone coughs, but the noise gives place to an abrupt silence. Those still waiting outside drape their bodies over the long rails of the bus stop shelter, and the lights of passing vehicles play upon their shapes in strange, desolate patterns. When the conductor returns he is eating a shiny loaf of bread by hollowing it out, and the food handled in this way in the darkness looks intermittently like something resentful and alive. With a full mouth the conductor shouts abuse at those who have climbed inside; a morsel shoots out from his jaws and drops in a pale arc by the bus.

'Get down! Get down! Have you paid and you are sitting inside?'

As if they have been expecting this all along, the people inside climb meekly down and hold out their money to the conductor. He is too angry to accept it, and sends them back to the end of the line. Nothing serious. The line is not long. The conductor mumbles insults aimed at no particular person as he snaps out the tickets. No one seems to need change, so things go rapidly, except when the conductor takes his time to say aloud some deeply felt insult.

The man gets in, choosing a seat by a window. The window turns out to have no pane in it. No matter. It is hardly a cold night. When the bus starts the air that rushes in comes like a soft wave of lukewarm water. The man leans back against his seat and fingers recoil behind his head. He does not look back. It is possible, after so much time up and down the same way, it is possible to close the eyes and lay back the head and yet to know very clearly that one is at this moment passing by that particular place or the other one, because the air brings these places to the open nose. Even at night there is something hot and dusty about the wind that comes blowing over the grease of the loco yard, so that the combination raises in the mind pictures of thick short men in overalls thickened with grease that never come off; blunt rusty bits of iron mixed up with filings in the sand; old water that has stopped flowing and confused itself with decaying oil from broken-down boilers; even the dead smell of carbide lamps and electric cutters. After the wall of the loco yard, the breeze blowing freely in from the sea, fresh in a special organic way that has in it traces of living things from their beginnings to their endings. Over the iron bridge the bus moves slowly. In gusts the heat rises from the market abandoned to the night and to the homeless, dust and perpetual mud covered over with crushed tomatoes and rotten vegetables, eddies from the open end of some fish head on a dump of refuse and curled-up scales with the hardening corpses of the afternoon's flies around. Another stretch of free sea line. More than half-way now, the world around the central rubbish heap is entered, and smells hit the senses like a strong wall, and even the eyes have something to register. It is so old it has become more than mere rubbish, that is why. It has fused with the earth underneath. In one or two places the eye that chooses to remain open can see the weird patterns made by thrown wrecks of upended bicycles and a prewar roller. Sounds arise and kill all smells as the bus pulls into the dormitory town. Past the big public lavatory the stench claws inward to the throat. Sometimes it is understandable that people spit so much, when all around decaying things push inward and mix all the body's juices with the taste of rot. Sometimes it is understandable, the doomed attempt to purify the self by adding to the disease outside. Hot smell of caked shit split by afternoon's baking sun, now touched by still evaporating dew. The nostrils, incredibly, are joined in a way that is most horrifying direct to the throat itself and to the entrails right through to their end. Across the aisle on the seat opposite, an old man is sleeping

40

and his mouth is open to the air rushing in the night with how many particles of what? So why should he play the fool and hold his breath? Sounds of moist fish frying in open pans of dark perennial oil so close to the public lavatory. It is very easy to get used to what is terrible. A different thing; the public bath, made for a purification that is not so offensive. Here there is only the stale soapsuds merging in grainy rotten dirt from everybody's scum, a reminder of armpits full of yellowed hair dripping sweat down arms raised casually in places of public intimacy. The bus whines up a hill and the journey is almost over. Here are waves of spice from late pots of familiar homes, spices to cover what strong meats?

The man gets down and his hands find their own way deep into his pockets. The air around the spine at the base of his neck grows unaccountably cold. The puddle at the end of the gutter is widening so that it takes some effort to leap over it now. And it seems such a tiring thing to do, climbing up the four little stairs on to the veranda. There is light in the kitchen still, but everything is very quiet. Is that strange at this time of night? It does not matter, really. Why should there not be silence, after all, why not?

Silence. No voices, no sounds in the night, just silence. The man walks into the hall, meeting the eyes of his waiting wife. These eyes are flat, the eyes of a person who has come to a decision not to say anything; eyes totally accepting and unquestioning in the way only a thing from which nothing is ever expected can be accepted and not questioned. And it is true that because these eyes are there the air is filled with accusation, but for even that the man feels a certain tired gratitude; he is thankful there are no words to lance the tension of the silence. The children begin to come out of the room within. They are not asleep, not even the third little one. It seems their eyes also are learning this flat look that is a defense against hope, as if their mother's message needs their confirmation. It comes across very well. So well it fills the hall with an unbearable heaviness which must be broken at all costs. The table has food on it. The man moves forward and sits at it with his back to his guilt, resolving to break the heavy quiet.

'I saw Koomson on my way home,' he says. The wife is slow about showing any interest.

'And Estella was with him, I suppose?' she asks at last.

'Uh-huh,' he nods, turning to look at her. He sees instead the eyes of his children. O you loved ones, spare your beloved the silent agony of your eyes.

'Mmmmmmmm.' The sound she makes should mean approval or at least acceptance, but it does not. Now it is a low cry full of resentment and disappointment. Then, 'She has married well . . .' The man wishes he had learned to bear the weight of the silence before, but now going back is impossible.

'They were going to the Atlantic-Caprice.' He raised the spoon to his mouth, and as he did so he caught the scent of perfume still on his hand. 'I shook hands with his wife, and I can smell her still. Her hand was wet with the stuff.'

'Mmmmmm.' This long sound again. 'Life has treated her well.'

'Koomson says he wants to come and see us. Sunday, nine.'

'Mmmmmmmm.'

'That probably means your mother, not us. We should remember to tell her when she comes.'

The woman paused before answering. 'It is not only for my mother that Koomson will come.'

'What do you mean?' asked the man. His spoon drops and he ignores it.

'I mean if things go well, they will go well for all of us.'

'Do you think so?' The man looks worriedly at his wife. She is irritated.

'Why are you trying to cut yourself apart from what goes for all of us?'

'I did not know,' the man says very slowly, 'I did not know that I had agreed to join anything.'

'But you will be eating it with us when it is ripe?' The woman's defensive little smile does nothing to remove the sharp edge of the question. The man rises from the table and goes toward his wife. She is about to shrink back from him, but he is smiling sadly down at her and she relaxes.

42

'Where is Koomson getting all the money for this boat?' he asks.

'He is getting it.' Flat finality.

'All right,' says the man. 'Let us say I am not in it.'

The woman stares unbelieving at her husband, then whispers softly, 'Chichidodooooo.'

Knock on the door. Answer from the woman, and an old woman with her breast barely covered by her cloth comes in holding a little chipped enamel bowl at the tips of her fingers.

'Good evening,' she says. 'Here I am again. Sugar. Would you be pleased to lend me a little sugar? Just for the children.'

The wife answers, 'We have just finished our last packet ourselves.'

On the old woman's face appears a smile halfway between scepticism and triumphant belief. As she disappears through the doorway she looks at the couple within and says, 'Ah, this life!'

The man looks at his wife and finds her eyes fixed on his face. 'What were you saying?' he asks.

'Nothing,' she says. He grows silent.

'Somebody offered me a bribe today,' he says after a while.

'Mmmmmmm!'

'One of those timber contractors.'

'Mmmmmmm. To do what?'

'To get him an allocation.'

'And like an Onward Christian Soldier you refused?'

The sudden vehemence of the question takes the man completely by surprise. 'Like a what?'

'On-ward Chris-tian Soooooooldier!
   Maaarching as to Waaaaaaaaar
With the Cross of Jeeeeeesus
   Goooing on be-foooooore!'

The man took a long look at his wife's face. Then he said, 'It wasn't even necessary.'

'What were you afraid of then?' the woman asked.

'But why should I take it?'

'And why not? When you shook Estella Koomson's hand, was not the perfume that stayed on yours a pleasing thing? Maybe you like this crawling that we do, but I am tired of it. I would like to have someone drive me where I want to go.'

'Like Estella Koomson?'

'Yes, like Estella. And why not? Is she more than I?'

'We don't know how she got what she has,' the man said.

'And we don't care.' The woman's voice had lost its excitement and reverted to its flatness. With a silent gesture she sent the children back inside. 'We don't care. Why pretend? Everybody is swimming toward what he wants. Who wants to remain on the beach asking the wind, "How ... How ... How?" '

'Is that the way you see things now?' he asked her.

'Have you found some other way?'

'No.'

'Would you refuse Koomson's car if it got given free to you?'

'No. I would depend ...'

'Is there anything wrong with some entertainment now and then?'

'Of course not.'

'Then why not?'

'Why not what?' he asked.

The woman's mouth opened, but she let it close again. Then she said, 'It is nice. It is clean, the life Estella is getting.'

The man shrugged his shoulders. Then he spoke, it was with deliberate laziness. 'Some of that kind of cleanness has more rottenness in it than the slime at the bottom of a garbage dump.'

'Mmmmmmm ...' the woman almost sang. The sound might have been taken as a murmur of contentment. 'You are the chichidodo itself.'

'Now what do you mean by that?' The man's voice was not angry, just intrigued. Very calmly, the woman gave him her reply.

'Ah, you know, the chichidodo is a bird. The chichidodo hates excrement with all its soul. But the chichidodo only feeds on maggots, and you know the maggots grow best inside the lavatory. This is the chichidodo.'

The woman was smiling.

CHAPTER FIVE

The reproach of loved ones comes kindly when it comes in silence. Even when this silence is filled with the consciousness of resentment there is always the hope that they understand whatever vague little wishes there are to understand, as if one could forever keep up the pretense that the difference between the failures and the hard heroes of the dream is only a matter of time. Time in which to leap across yards made up of the mud of days of rain; to jump over wide gutters with only a trickle of drying urine at the bottom and so many clusters of cigarette pieces wet and pinched in where they have left the still unsatisfied lips of the sucker. Time to sail with a beautiful smoothness in the sweet direction of the gleam, carrying with easy strength every one of the loved ones; time to change the silent curses of resentful loved ones and the deeper silent questions of those in whom pain and disappointment have killed every other emotion, time to change all this into the long unforced laughter of tired travellers home at last. But when the reproach of the loved ones grow into sound and the pain is thrown outward against the one who causes it, then it is no longer possible to look with any hope at all at time.

The man moved from the table and lay down on the bed pushed into the far corner of the hall and closed his eyes, but failure would not let him rest in peace. Arguments and counter-accusations that had run many times round and round just underneath the surface of his mind now rose teasingly and vanished again beneath his confusion after they had multiplied it and deepened it beyond the point where it could be endured. A man, even a man who has stumbled once, ought to be able to pick himself up and hurry after those who have gone before, a man ought to be able to do that, if only for the sake of the loved ones. And the man also who in his stumbling is pressed down with burdens other than his own, he also must hurry. The

46

judgement of the loved ones is no different from the judgement of the others, though in the lonely mind the loved ones may themselves look like a strong excuse for the failure and the fall. What would be the point, when so much pain was shooting out toward, the beloved, what would be the point in his returning it? What would be the point, especially since these days outside the area of the gleam which made the loved ones suffer in their impatience, there was nothing worth pursuing, nothing at all worth spending life's minutes on?

There was nothing the man could say to his wife, and the woman herself did not look as if she thought there could be anything said to her about what she knew was so true. But inside the man the confusion and the impotence had swollen into something asking for a way out of confinement, and in his restlessness he rose and went out very quietly through the door, and his wife sat there not even staring after him, not even asking where he was going or when he would come back in the night, or even whether he wanted to return at all to this home.

Outside, the night was a dark tunnel so long that out in front and above there never could be any end to it, and to the man walking down it it was plain that the lights here and there illuminated nothing so strongly as they did the endless power of the night, easily, softly calling every sleeping thing into itself. Looking all around him the man saw that he was the only thing that had no way of answering the call of the night. His eyes were hurting in their wakefulness, and in this night air that was moist with the water and the salt of the sea nearby, he felt a terrible dryness in his nostrils and in his mouth all the way down into his throat, and his head had grown heavy with too much lightness. Around a street lamp high over the coal tar, insects of the night whirled in a crazy dance, drawn not directly by the night from which they had come, but by the fire of the lamps in it. Their own way of meeting the night, and it was all the same in the end. Was there not something in the place and about the time, everything, in fact, that sought to make it painfully clear that there was too much of the unnatural in any man who imagines he could escape the inevitable decay of life and not accept the decline into final disintegration? Against the all too natural, such struggles – could they be anything but the perverse attempts of desperate hedonists to perpetuate their youth against the impending rot of age? A friend remembered, Rama Krishna. A Ghanaian, but he had taken that far-off name in the reincarnation of his soul after long and tortured flight from everything close and everything known, since all around him showed him the horrible threat of decay. Soul eaten up with thoughts of evergreen things and of an immortality he was always striving to understand, the friend had plunged with all his body into the yoga others take to be a mere aid to this life. Meditative exercises and special diets of honey and of vinegar, and a firm, sad refusal to kill any living thing for food. 'Yes,' he would agree with any who asked, 'it is in the wisdom also that the silent plants, who knows, may be more alive than the destroyed souls, we who consume them.' Then solemnly, like a man in great distress of spirit, he would go to another book of another stranger whom he called sometimes the Prophet and sometimes Gibran, and read:

> Would that you could live on the fragrance of the earth,
> and like an air plant be sustained by the light.
> But since you must kill to eat,
> And rob the newly born of its mother's milk to quench your thirst,
> let it then be an act of worship . . .

But it could be seen that these words that were meant to put a lost serenity into the spirit of the questioner never were able to put at rest the grieving soul of the friend. Near the end he had discovered the one way: he would not corrupt himself by touching any woman, but saved his semen to rejuvenate his brain by standing on his head a certain number of minutes every night and every dawn. Everywhere he wore a symbolic evergreen and a faraway look on his face, thinking of the escape from corruption and of immortality. It was of consumption that he died, so very young, but already his body inside had undergone far more decay than any living body, however old and near death, can expect to see. It was whispered – how indeed are such things ever known? – that the disease had completely eaten up the frail matter of his lungs, and that where his heart ought to have been there was only a living lot of worms gathered together tightly in the shape of a heart. And so what did the dead rot inside the friend not have to do with his fear of what was decaying outside of himself? And what would such an unnatural flight be worth at all, in the end? And the man wondered what kind of sound the cry of the chichidodo bird could be, the bird longing for its maggots but fleeing the feces which gave them birth.

Crossing over to the side of the main connecting road nearer the sea, the man walked the whole distance to the Essei area, keeping just behind the breakwater that kept the sea from destroying the road. Now and then the headlights of some oncoming vehicle came and blinded him and afterward the darkness of the night was even deeper and more infinite than before, so that a little of the lost comfortable feeling of the man alone in the world outside, so unlike the loneliness of the beloved surrounded by the grieving loved ones, came back to him in little frustrating sweet moments that were gone before they could be grasped. And yet, in some region of his mind, the thought almost rose: that it should not really be possible for the guiltless to feel so beaten down with the accusation of those so near . . . but the thought was never really able to come to the surface, and dipped downward again as swiftly as it had come, leaving only dissatisfaction. At the bridge, the lagoon to the left stood out by being even darker than the surrounding darkness itself, and the lights on it of the night fishermen going home came all the way over as very long, very thin shimmers that never ceased to surprise the eye. Near the Essei market the long row of small windows where the prostitutes lived had a strange beauty, and from one of the rooms there came a long, happy laugh that ended as if the young woman who had laughed so long had grown quite exhausted with the effort.

Some time ago – how long ago? – it was said the Essei market and the whole area around it had been another lagoon. Even now, after a day of heavy rain, sometimes the big drain became a swift river and the market was nothing but a shallow lake until the water could go down back into the earth or to the sea or into the air again. And even then the earth of the market always kept a softness that gave an unusual silence to the walker's footfalls. Around the market loose groups of Frafra and Hausa men sat selling penny loaves and tea in old milk cans, though there were no buyers around this time of night. Now the walls of corrugated iron slid past in dim waves of light. Occasionally there was a thick mud-and-cement wall with bulky iron grating outlined against the light from inside. On the ground lazy water searched fruitlessly for gutters in which to flow, finally giving up in puddles whose scum was visible even in the dark.

The sweet sadness of Congo music flowed out through a window near the end of a row of little houses, and the man stopped there. Holding on to the upright window bars, he looked into the room. Inside, on a small bed pushed against the far wall next to the door, a man lay reading. The man outside stood a long time at the window, holding on to the iron bars and looking quietly at the naked man within. Then he walked the remaining distance to the gate of the house, crossed the little yard, and knocked on the door of the naked man's room. The door opened silently and he entered. The naked man did not get up. He looked up momentarily from his book, then with an easy smile he went back to his reading. The man did not disturb him. On the radio two announcers, a man and a woman, read out a long list of names that sounded at once very far away and very African, and then another of those sad harmonies came floating outward from the little set. The man moved to the opposite side of the room and sat down on the desk against the wall, resting his feet on the chair near it.

The music stopped on a long chord which lingered even after the twin voices had said what must have been their farewells to unseen listeners, and lost itself in the repeated tinkle of the sound signal that followed. The naked man on the bed reached out with his left hand and turned the tuning knob. Sounds like the swift bumps of waves hitting returning waves, pierced by other sounds, high, sharp, and very brief. Then the sound of a song hurriedly crossed and returned to. The reception had been good, but now it was even clearer. The closest station, Radio Ghana. The song was a very ordinary 'high life', but before the hand could turn the knob it had ended and another, slower, softer song was on the air. The man on the bed took his hand gently back and closed the book he had been reading, listening to the miracle. It was a very slow song, though every hole in it was filled with sounds that said too painfully much to the listening ear, and when the words began, from the mouths of singers who must have felt it all together, they only added to what was there already, like the rain that comes after a long day when all the air is filled with heat and with wetness.

> Those who are blessed with the power
> And the soaring swiftness of the eagle
> And have flown before,
> Let them go.
> I will travel slowly,
> And I too will arrive.

Visibly, the song deepened the silence of the man on the bed. For the man sitting on the desk opposite, all the cool sadness seemed able to do was to raise thoughts of the lonely figure finding it more and more difficult to justify his own honesty. How could he, when all around him the whole world never tired of saying there were only two types of men who took refuge in honesty – the cowards and the fools? Very often these days he was burdened with the hopeless, impotent feeling that he was not just one of these, but a hopeless combination of the two. Thoughts and images rose of the lonely man trapped at a bar, who does not drink but feels far more confused than all the masquerading drinkers, and when the images came closer to merge with his own self, he was the careful man refusing to gamble with his life, and therefore feeling the keen-eyed reproach of those closest to himself. And all the time the eyes that could never be avoided just stared steadily and made it terrifyingly plain that in these times honesty could only be a social vice, for the one who chose to indulge in it nothing but a very hostile form of selfishness, a very perverse selfishness.

> And have climbed in haste,
> Let them go.
> I will journey softly,
> But I too will arrive.

Someone must have felt something very deeply to have cried out these long sounds of despair refusing to die. How many people had life itself brought to such an understanding without their knowing it? How long would it last against the beckoning power of the gleam and the terrible push of the powerless hunger of the loved ones? Slow, suspended notes dying toward the end, then faded out too sharply leaving inside a frustration very much like physical hunger. In the momentary silence following, the naked man on the bed sighs, throws out his hand again turning the knob, but the search produces nothing but harsh wireless voices, and so he turns the whole thing off. From the desk the man watches, and when he sees that the other has not gone back to his book, he begins to speak to him.

'I did not know about that one.'

'No. First time I heard it was this morning.'

'I wonder who dreamed it up,' said the man.

'Yes,' his companion answered, 'I'd like to know. A few people are seeing things and saying them. I'd like to know.'

'I hear the bands make up their own songs.'

'Poets who have failed.'

'Why?'

'I shouldn't have said that, really. It should be the other way round.'

'Poets are bandleaders who have failed?'

'Something like that.'

'And ourselves?'

Question bounces off unheeded as the naked man gets up off the bed, takes a pencil from the top of the bookcase near the bed and sticks it in to mark his page. He puts the book on the case and sits back down on the bed, pushing his back against the head and drawing up his knees.

'What is that?' asks the man on the desk, indicating the book.

'I saw it yesterday. It was the title that interested me. *He Who Must Die*. Greek writer.'

'Is it good?'

'Very. There are so many good things we don't get a chance to see. They have to get translated first. And even then . . .'

The man on the desk said nothing for a while, then, 'People can see you like this from your window.'

'If they care to stop and look. It doesn't worry me.' The man on the desk chuckled feebly.

'So.' The man on the bed spoke again. Not a question, not a statement.

'I wanted to come and see you,' the man said.

The listener shook his head reprovingly: 'Running from family peace again.'

'It's serious, this time.'

'It's serious, every time.'

'You can laugh,' the man said.

'You really think so?' asked the naked man. 'You really think I can afford to laugh?' He was smiling.

'Well,' the man said, 'you have not made the most serious mistake.'

The naked man laughed out loud. 'You wouldn't want my life, I tell you.'

'Teacher, you reduce everything to a joke.'

'I am sorry. That is not my intention.' There was a note of real unhappiness in the voice now, and the man on the desk looked down at the cement floor beneath his feet.

'Oyo flung my uselessness at me again this night,' he said.

'What happened?'

'She called me the chichidodo.'

'Ah. It's a proverb, no? The bird eats shit, hates worms?'

'Yes. Only the other way round, Teacher.'

'Why did she say that?'

'I told her what happened at work today. A man came to me with a bribe.'

'And murderer that you are, you let it go?'

53

'I let it go,' the man said.

'Expect no forgiveness from your family, then.'

'I understand you,' said the man. 'I understand you with my mind when you speak so coldly about this thing. But people want so much.'

'They want what they see others enjoying, that is all.'

'And it doesn't matter how they get it?'

'It doesn't matter. There are ways and ways. You, the husband, will have to find these ways. It is very simple, isn't it?'

'You know,' said the man, 'that in the end there is only one way. Only one way for people like us.'

'Well, then.'

'Well, then, what, Teacher?'

'Are you so surprised when your people are angry with you for not taking the one way open to them?'

'Ah, but that one way!'

'Exactly!' said the naked man. 'That one way is a path you want to avoid. What will your people do, then? Pretend they have no desires?'

'They will destroy me, Teacher.'

'Or make you a big man. One of the two, who knows?'

The man closed his eyes and let his feet swing underneath him. They barely missed the floor.

'What I don't understand,' he said, 'is my own feeling about it. I know I have done nothing wrong. I could even get angry with Oyo about this. And yet, and yet I am the one who feels strange.'

'The condemned man.'

'Yes. I feel like a criminal. Often these days I find myself thinking of something sudden I could do to redeem myself in their eyes. Then I sit down and ask myself what I have done wrong, and there is really nothing.'

'You have not done what everybody is doing,' said the naked man, 'and in this world that is one of the crimes. You have always known that.'

The man on the desk stopped swinging his legs and looked at his friend. 'If she hates me that much,' he said, 'why does she remain with me?'

'Where could she go?' the naked man asked. 'Besides you are exaggerating things. After all, for a married insult, this chichidodo proverb was very mild.'

'You used to speak more kindly, Teacher.'

'I am sorry.'

The man on the desk sat looking downward at his suspended feet. The naked man turned his face toward him and waited for him to speak.

'When the time comes that Teacher also just laughs at my pain, where will I be going next?'

'I was not laughing at you,' said the naked man. 'I was thinking of your wife. A very polite woman, your wife,' he said, and the laugh that followed was dry and far too long. 'I feel as if she had said those words to me too. I suppose we are all that.'

'All what?'

'All chichidodos, those of us whose entrails are not hard enough for the national game.'

'I never heard you talk much about it,' the man said.

'It is not my habit, that is true. I have spent so much time running from it.'

'I thought you were one person entirely free of all this.'

'No. I have tried to be free, but I am not free. Perhaps I will never even be.' The naked man turned on his side and propped himself on his right elbow, facing the man on the desk. 'It was all so good, the youth and the thoughts of honest living water flowing to thirsty land, wasn't it? But what happens when you come out and you see the land wants you, not honest and living, but completely like its dead self? You didn't think I too had wondered about that?'

'I think of you as the freest person I know,' said the man.

'Then everyone you know is a slave.'

'You have escaped the call of the loved ones, as you say.'

'Yes but I am not free. I have not stopped wanting to meet the loved ones and to touch them and be touched by them. But you know that the loved ones are dead even when they walk around the earth like the living, and you know that all they want is that you throw away the thing in your mind that makes you think you are still alive, and their embrace will be a welcome unto death.'

'And so Teacher runs.'

'And so I run. I know I am nothing and will never be anything without them, and when most I wish to stop being nothing, then the desire to run back to those I have fled comes back with unbearable strength. Until I see again those loving arms outstretched, bringing me their gift of death. Then I stop and turn around and come back here, living my half-life of loneliness.'

'But it is what you have yourself chosen,' replies the man. 'Is that not far better?'

'Better? Wandering . . . nothing . . . it depends. But, you see; it is not a choice between life and death, but what kind of death we can bear, in the end. Have you not seen there is no salvation anywhere?'

'My wife thinks there is.'

'There is salvation of some kind, of course,' said the naked man, 'but only within the cycle of our damnation itself.'

'You talk like one of these new believers, Teacher.'

'The believers have the clearest words.'

'My wife has seen the true salvation.'

'How do you know?'

'She talks about it, Teacher. It is the blinding gleam of beautiful new houses and the shine of powerful new Mercedes cars. It is also the scent of expensive perfumes and the mass of a new wig.'

'Money, you mean.'

'Yes, Teacher,' the man said, 'money, but not only money. Power, too. And these days it is all coming together in the person of Koomson.'

'Careful, man. Big names must not be mentioned naked. His Excellency Joseph Koomson, Minister Plenipotentiary, Member of the Presidential Commission, Hero of Socialist Labor. Is that the dignitary you mean?'

'My wife and her mother think he is about to make them rich.'

'Well, maybe he is.'

56

'Something about a boat. The way Oyo's mother tells it, he is just going to buy a lot of fishing boats and give them to her.'

'Excellent. Excellent, man. Remember me when the fish comes.'

'Koomson is just going to fool them.'

'You don't know, man. Just close your mouth and watch.'

'But I know!' the man shouted.

'All right, then. Go and say it. Your wife will hate you for it, and her mother will speak to you of envy.'

'But, Teacher, I cannot sit and watch Oyo and her mother getting fooled by this Koomson, can I?'

'Why not? I would advise you to do exactly that. Let them do what they want. Maybe they will get rich. You don't know how to make them rich, so let them try.'

'How would you feel?'

'Man, forget about how you feel. If you prevent your wife and her mother from getting their fishing boats, you will have two enemies close to you for the rest of your life.'

The man slid off the desk. He began pacing aimlessly about the room, stopping as he came to each wall to support himself against it.

'They are using this boat thing, Teacher,' he said. 'They are using it to hit me on the head every terrible day, to make me feel so useless. And the bad thing is I know they have succeeded. I am asking myself what is wrong with me. Do I have some part missing? Teacher, this Koomson was my own classmate. My classmate, Teacher, my classmate. So tell me, what is wrong with me?'

'It may be that you cannot lie very well, and you are afraid to steal. That is what is wrong with you. Any more headaches?'

'Some time ago I could see it like that,' the man said. 'But these days I say to myself that that is only childish. I used to get some strength for another day when I could see it like that.'

'What has happened to change your way of seeing things?'

'Oyo.'

'Why, is she expecting another baby?'

'That is not it. That's not it at all.'

'So what else did she do?'

'She told me about her way of looking at these things. From that day even the strength I used to call up to support myself has vanished.' The man moved away from the wall and stopped just in front of the bookcase, as if he were looking for some title there. But his words did not stop.

'One fine day Oyo explained everything to me. I think it was when this boat scheme was first mentioned. I had asked Oyo's mother who would pay for the boats, and with a great deal of pride she said the Minister would. Which Minister? Koomson, of course. Only she called him Brother Joe. Brother! Aaah, so. I said I didn't know Koomson had enough money to buy even one boat. Those thing cost thousands and thousands of cedis. My mother-in-law asked me very patiently whether I did not know also that Brother Joe had influence. She called it infruence. I had taken a piece of paper to calculate Koomson's total salary since he joined the Party. Now I dropped the paper and said, "Oh, I see." And again with this patience of hers my mother-in-law asked me what I had seen at last. So I got angry enough to tell her I had seen corruption. Public theft.'

'You were very ill-mannered. Upatriotic, in fact.'

'My mother-in-law walked out of my house.'

'Good. Down with subversive elements who attack the nation's fabric.'

'For some reason I had expected Oyo to agree with me. I was wrong. When her mother left she began to talk to me about her life, and I thought she had been finding new ways to make our marriage more interesting. Like philosophy.'

'You should have been a priest. You have such kind thoughts.'

'Teacher, my wife explained to me, step by step, that life was like a lot of roads: long roads, short roads, wide and narrow, steep and level, all sorts of roads. Next, she let me know that human beings were like so many people driving their cars on all these roads. This was the point at which she told me that those who wanted to get far had to learn to drive fast. And then she asked me what name I would give to people who were afraid to drive fast, or to drive at all. I had no name to give her, but she had not finished. Accidents would happen, she told me, but the fear of accidents would never keep men from driving, and Joe Koomson had learned to drive.'

'Allow me to foretell your future, friend. With a wife like that, you will not only be rich. You will be great very soon.'

'I will remember you, Teacher. But can't you see the truth in what she said?'

'I can see it.' The naked man laughed. 'I have seen it so clearly I have spent a long time running from it.'

'She was right, but it was not philosophy she was talking about. It was Ghana.'

'The accidents are those who get caught.'

'That is so right, Teacher,' the man said, 'and the driver is me.'

'And the driver is you.'

'From that day I have not been able to stop wondering what went wrong with me, and where. Koomson was my classmate.'

'You say that like a litany.'

'He was not very intelligent.' The man was pacing the room again. 'Shit, he was actually stupid.'

'So maybe he got a new brain.'

'New brain my foot,' the man said. 'But that is what my people will not see. Koomson is doing very well for himself. . . . These days any young man with brains can do very well. . . . They make me feel like a criminal.'

'They are only urging you to get ahead. They like you, no?'

'You can talk like that. You are lucky.'

'You have no idea what a horrible thing loneliness can be.'

'Teacher, you chose to be alone.'

'Only because I can't drive.'

'You have all your freedom.'

'That makes me far more of a criminal than you. You see me in the daytime and you think I am free. Perhaps you even imagine I am happy. So keep thinking that. It may give you something to hope for. But I tell you, those I have fled visit me in my dreams. There is my mother. Now at last she leaves me alone, but two nights past she was with me in a dream full of guilt and fear and loneliness. I had come to a place much like the area around the courthouse in the Bakano neighborhood of Cape Coast. Near the old government school there was a big mansion, like a castle, painted a soft white color with a shade of brown mixed up in it. The castle, in my dream, belonged to my mother. With a companion who shared all my soul's desires I had come from a long way off, seeking refuge with my mother in her house. The mansion was very large. There was room, lots of room, in it, but when I spoke to my mother she seemed torn within by an impossible decision. But then she made up her mind, and out of her ran a stream of words, every drop filled with all the resentment and the hate of her long disappointment with me. "Yes, you have come to rest here, you who have put nothing here at all. So how much money have you given me in all your life, and how much help? And now you come here, here, here." When her anger grew unbearable she drove me out into the street outside. I walked a little way and soon I found myself in a place with houses bigger and darker than any I had ever seen, streets wider and emptier than any here, and people I had never known could exist in this world. Do you still think I am a happy man?'

'We all have our dreams,' the man said.

'And our troubles, too. How can I think I am doing the right thing when I am alone and there are so many I have run from? Who is right at all? I know I have chosen something, but it is not something I would have chosen if I had the power to choose truly. I am just sitting there, and if you think I am happier than you driving out there, you just don't know what I feel inside. I had so much hope before . . . so much hope . . .'

'I am not even sure I ever had that,' the man said.

'Oh, you are forgetting things in your unhappiness.'

'You are right. All I remember clearly these days is that I have been walking along paths chosen for me before I had really decided, and it makes me feel the way I think impotent men feel. You can't tell me you feel the same way. You have this freedom, Teacher. You have your freedom.'

'It makes no difference. If we can't consume ourselves for something we believe in, freedom makes no difference at all. You see, I am free to do what I want, but there is nothing happening now that I want to join. There used to be something, and you know what I mean.'

'I know.' The man paused, then, as if he had come to something altogether different, he said, 'You're still hoping, aren't you, Teacher?'

'Hoping for what?'

'Anything. An end to this ... a beginning to something else. Anything?'

'No. Not any more. Not hope, anyhow. I don't feel any hope in me any more. I can see things, but I don't feel much. When you can see the end of things even in their beginnings, there's no more hope, unless you want to pretend, or forget, or get drunk or something. No. I also am one of the dead people, the walking dead. A ghost. I died long ago. So long ago that not even the old libations of living blood will make me live again.'

The naked man turned on his bed. He turned the left knob on the radio till it would go no farther, and then gave the tuning knob an inward pull that slid the red line smoothly across the glass face. When it stopped a male voice, huge like a eunuch amplified, burst the air with a hollered sound that kept its echo long afterward, a vibrating '... ericaaaaa!' while underneath the aggressive, scrambled loudness of music from across the ocean took over the room. The naked man calmly switched off the sound, lay with his full length on his back, his arms raised and bent so that he could support his resting head in his open palms, and relaxed all over, looking only at the ceiling.

Opposite him, the man went very quietly back to the desk and sat on it, just thinking, looking, and listening.

CHAPTER SIX

Why do we waste so much time with sorrow and pity for ourselves? It is true now that we are men, but not so long ago we were helpless messes of soft flesh and unformed bone squeezing through bursting motherholes, trailing dung and exhausted blood. We could not ask then why it was necessary for us also to grow. So why now should we be shaking our head and wondering bitterly why there are children together with the old, why time does not stop when we ourselves have come to stations where we would like to rest? It is so like a child, to wish all movement to cease.

And yet the wondering and the shaking and the vomiting horror is not all from the inward sickness of the individual soul. Here we have had a kind of movement that should make even good stomachs go sick. What is painful to the thinking mind is not the movement itself, but the dizzying speed of it. It is that which has been horrible. Unnatural, I would have said, had I not stopped myself with asking, unnatural according to what kind of nature? Each movement and each growth, each such thing brings with itself its own nature to frustrate our future judgement. Now, whenever I am able to look past the beauty of the first days, the days of birth, I can see growth. I tell myself that is the way it should be. There is nothing that should break the heart in the progressive movement away from the beauty of the first days. I see growth, that is all I see within my mind. When I can only see, when there is nothing I can feel, I am not troubled. But always these unwanted feelings will come in the end and disturb the tired mind with thoughts that will not go away. How horribly rapid everything has been, from the days when men were not ashamed to talk of souls and of suffering and of hope, to these low days of smiles that will never again be sly enough to hide the knowledge of betrayal and deceit. There is something of an irresistible horror in such quick decay.

When I was at school, in Standard Five, one of us, a boy who took a special pleasure in showing us true but unexpected sides of our world, came and showed us something I am sure none of us has forgotten. We called him Aboliga the Frog. His eyes were like that. Aboliga the Frog one day brought us a book of freaks and oddities, and showed us his favorite among the weird lot. It was a picture of something the caption called an old manchild. It had been born with all the features of a human baby, but within seven years it had completed the cycle from babyhood to infancy to youth, to maturity and old age, and in its seventh year it had died a natural death. The picture Aboliga the Frog showed us was of the manchild in its gray old age, completely old in everything save the smallness of its size, a thing that deepened the element of the grotesque. The manchild looked more irretrievably old, far more thoroughly decayed, than any ordinary old man could ever have looked. But of course, it, too, had a nature of its own, so that only those who have found some solid ground they can call the natural will feel free to call it unnatural. And where is my solid ground these days? Let us say just that the cycle from birth to decay has been short. Short, brief. But otherwise not at all unusual. And even in the decline into the end there are things that remind the longing mind of old beginnings and hold out the promise of new ones, things even like your despair itself. I have heard this pain before, only then it was multiplied many, many times, but that may only be because at that time I was not so alone, so far apart. Maybe there are other lonely voices despairing now. I will not be entranced by the voice, even if it should swell as it did in the days of hope. I will not be entranced, since I have seen the destruction of the promises it made. But I shall not resist it either. I will be like a cork.

It is so surprising, is it not, how even the worst happenings of the past acquire a sweetness in the memory. Old harsh distresses are now merely pictures and tastes which hurt no more, like itching scars which can only give pleasure now. Strange, because when I can think soberly about it all, without pushing any later joys into the deeper past, I can remember that things were terrible then.

When the war was over the soldiers came back to homes broken in their absence and they themselves brought murder in their hearts and gave it to those nearest them. I saw it, not very clearly, because I had no way of understanding it, but it frightened me. We had gone on marches of victory and I do not think there was anyone mean enough in spirit to ask whether we knew the thing we were celebrating. Whose victory? Ours? It did not matter. We marched, and only a dishonest fool will look back on his boyhood and say he knew even then that there was no meaning in any of it. It is so funny now, to remember that we all thought we were welcoming victory. Or perhaps there is nothing funny here at all, and it is only that victory itself happens to be the identical twin of defeat.

There was the violence, first of all. If that was not something entirely new, at any rate the frequency and the intensity of it were new things. No one before had told me of so many people going away to fight and coming back with blood and money eating up their minds. And afterward, those who might have answered me if I had asked them before would not take any notice of me, so busy were they all with looking and wondering what it was all about, and when it would end, and if it would end at all. There were no answers then. There never will be any answers. What will a man ever do when he is called to show his manhood fighting in alien lands and leaving his women behind with the demented and the old and the children and the other women? What will a man ever do but think his women will remain his even though he is no longer there with them? And what will a woman do for absent men who send back money not to be spent but to be kept for unknown times when they hope to return, if return they ever will? What new thing is money if it is not to be spent? So there were men who, against the human wishes of some women they had married in their youth, did not die in foreign lands but came back boldly, like drunken thieves in blazing afternoons and cold nights, knowing before they had even drunk the water with the lying smile of welcome that they had been betrayed. Their anger came out in the blood of those closest to themselves, these men who had gone without anger to fight enemies they did not even know; they found anger and murder waiting for them, lying in the bosoms of the women they had left behind. All that the young eye could see then was the truth; that the land had become a place messy with destroyed souls and lost bodies looking for something that could take their pain and finding nothing but those very people whose pain should have been their pain, and for whose protection they should have learned to fight, if there had been any reason left anywhere. It was also the time of the fashion of the jackknife and the chuke, the rapid unthinking movement of short, ugly iron points that fed wandering living ghosts with what they wanted, blood that would never put an end to their inner suffering.

A lot found it impossible to survive the destruction of the world they had carried away with them in their departing heads, and so they went simply mad, like Home Boy, endlessly repeating harsh, unintelligible words of command he had never understood but had learned to obey in other people's countries, marching all the day, everywhere, and driving himself to his insane exhaustion with the repetition of all the military drill he had learned, always to the proud accompaniment of his own scout whistle with its still-shiny metal sound. Some went very quietly into a silence no one could hope to penetrate, something so deep that it swallowed completely men who had before been strong: they just plunged into this deep silence and died. Those who were able picked up the pieces of shattered worlds and selves, swallowed all the keen knowledge of betrayal, and came with us along the wharves to search for some humiliating work that could give meaning to the continuing passage of unwelcome days; a hundred or so men waiting with eyes that had gotten lost in the past or in the future, always in some faraway place and time, any faraway place and time, provided it was not the horrible now and here, a hundred men waiting too quietly to fill places enough for seven.

Kofi Billy was one of the lucky ones, picked to do work that was too cruel for white men's hands. He did his work well. At the end of a day he was always tired, but he had found some sort of happiness in all of this, and that was something very valuable indeed. He was one day moving cargo, pushing it with his giant hands across some deck when somewhere some fresh young Englishman sitting at some machine loaded too much tension into even the steel ropes on board and one of them snapped. The free rope whipped with all that power through the air and just cut Kofi Billy's right leg away beneath the knee. He said for a long while he felt nothing at all, and then he felt everything a man could ever feel, and the world vanished for him. The Englishman said he deserved it: he had been playing at his work. Had he moved faster, he would not have been there when the steel rope snapped. Before him I had never actually known anybody with a wooden leg like that, and he himself was unwilling ever to talk about it. He just sat looking at the space which the wool-and-metal limb could never fill, and said nothing. Sister Maanan found refuge in lengthening bottles, and the passing foreigner gave her money and sometimes even love. The wharves turned men into gulls and vultures, sharp waiters for weird foreign appetites to satisfy, pilots of the hungry alien seeking human flesh. There were the fights, of course, between man and man, not so much over women as over white men asking to be taken to women, and the films brought the intelligent mind clever new fashions in dress and in murder. There were the more exciting, far more complete fights between large groups of violent men, when soldiers for some reason no one cared to know would be fighting policemen, or solid Kroo men would stand and fight the returned warriors. These were acts of violence directed outward. I do not believe that even this was fully half the horror we all felt. I know that my friends felt the way I felt. And what I felt inside was the approach of something much like death itself. The thing that would have killed us was that there was nothing to explain all this, nothing outside ourselves and those near us or those even weaker than ourselves that we could attack. There was no way out visible to us, and out on the hills the white men's gleaming bungalows were so far away, so unreachably far that people did not even think of them in their suffering. And for those who did, there were tales of white men with huge dogs that ate more meat in a single day than a human Gold Coast family got in a month, dogs which could obey their masters' voices like soldiers at war, and had as little love for black skins as their white masters.

*

The listening mind is disturbed by memories from the past. So much time has gone by, and still there is no sweetness here. Out on the road to school, the long lines of trees with little mangoes just growing on them, setting the impatient teeth on edge with their acid bite. And yet it was not possible to wait. There were so many children with so many hungers and desires. Stones flying upward and arcing down, bringing not the wanted fruit but entire bunches of unready mangoes. The sunshine feeling after a morning of short, unusually gentle rain, the water not yet dried up off the beautiful grass coming all the way down the long sides of white men's hills. Here and there the unbelievable smoothness of mounds of sand, the white people's playthings on the golf course. Occasionally the hurting inward dart of sunlight hitting small clear balls of water lingering on the green of grass and hibiscus plants and bouncing out and away into coming eyes and vanishing again. Three boys in khaki running races across and up the hill, with their suspenders falling over small shoulders. Irresistible rides down clean, smooth bottoms of gutters cutting down the hill to mix the unchanneled mud below with water. And the water coming from the hills was always clean, like unused water, or like water used by ghosts without flesh. So clean that at the bottom of the hills all the lepers used it for washing their clothes and for bathing their own sores, catching its cleanness before it reached the mud. Around the white bungalows on the hills no hungry children had thrown any stones and the mangoes that would long ago have disappeared hung heavy and ripe and beautiful, and the white men in the bungalows did not even want to eat them. The feel of sunlight on naked neck just above the khaki collar, and the short whistle of wet grass under naked feet making the climb up toward shiny white bungalows. Fences and hedges. Fences white and tall with wooden boards pointed and glinting in the sun, hedges thick and very high, their beautiful greenness not even covering their thorns. Looking for almonds, the white man's peanuts. Almonds big as mangoes, and some so ripe they had grown all red. Mangoes hanging big and gold, and outside eyes looking and longing. The third boy finds a hole down on the ground, underneath the hedge. Small hole, three boys, three khaki uniforms ruined with thorns and dirt. It seems maybe true that the white men are living ghosts themselves. For a place where people live, there is no sound here at all. But it is impossible to see inside, beyond the netting at all the windows. Nothing like a long pole lying around. Never throw stones around a white man's bungalow. So three little boys turn their backs to the white man's bungalow and bring down ripe mangoes with unripe ones fallen on the ground before. Keeping quiet. The white man, in case he exists, must not be waked up. Then sudden noises of footsteps within, moving out. Such a lot of mangoes and such big almonds to have to leave behind, and the hole is far too small and the thorns are cruelly sharp, coming through the khaki all the painful way into the flesh. The backward glance brings terror in the shape of two dogs, and they look much larger than any angry father. Down a steep hill it is easy to run fast but impossible to run well. Dogs are much faster anyhow. So much speed overturns the runner. In the midst of everything there is a filling satisfaction that a boy can run so fast sometimes. Even grass is painful when the face of a runner rubs hard against it and it yields unto the earth beneath. Does the dog actually bite, or is it no more interested in the fallen form, or can a dog also roll a child over and leave it feeling thoroughly beaten by life? Behind the dogs come tall black men in singlets, with long whips bending in their hands. The black men are truly angry, angrier than the dogs, and there is no mistake about the sharpness of their whips. Would it have been enough just to frighten three little boys away? That did not seem to be the point. The tall black men whipped like men in a struggle for life over death. Behind them the white man had come out and with a little white boy was watching calmly from the hill. The sun still shone so beautifully when it came off the white walls behind the white man, and three boys came together again and wondered whether it would be worse to go back or to go home.

*

The anger came out, but it was all victim anger that had to find even weaker victims, and it was never satisfied, always adding shame to itself. It is really so easy for a friend to begin treating a friend as a criminal to be feared. It is difficult to sit and see a friend with something you need desperately but do not have, it is difficult to sit and watch a friend keep this thing until the time comes when he will need it. There was nothing we could do, after robbing those who had been kind to us, except to lie down with the feeling that things were not right. It was like rushing down mossy bottoms of steep gutters from the hills with nothing to stop us. Only the gutters this time had no end, and the speed long before had become something far more than we could bear.

It had been possible to take to drink in the search for comforting darkness of the memory. In days when there was still something that could be stolen from the absent friend, it had been possible. But a time came when there was not enough anywhere around, and deep thought had to go into the spending of what there was. Man would just have broken up and gone crazy then, I suppose, but this was also the time that we found out about *wee*.

It was Sister Maanan who brought it to us one evening, saying it was the thing that had made her able to look at a bottle of Schnapps and say to herself that there was just another bottle of poison and pain. Yet she did not seem to be preaching, only offering us this thing we all felt we should have had before. The way Sister Maanan was getting it, it was not a thing that needed so much money, and yet instead of blinding us the way spirits would have done, it took us years beyond our old selves and made us see so many miles beyond all those old points. It used to amaze me afterwards that there was so much lying shit flying around about wee. It used to amaze me until I grew old enough to see that it is all very natural that judges willing to sit through hot afternoons sweating under foolish wigs should feel truly indignant when some poor bastard gets knocked into court for trying to see beyond the pain of the moment, smoking wee. Those among the judges who happen to be able to read know that all the holy anger is dog shit, pure and simple, anyway. They know wherever doctors have been asked before old judges let go of their bad breath, they have said the truth. Wee is far less dangerous than beer, and it is not only that it brings no headaches after it. I have not yet seen a man or woman who has smoked wee and who can look with anything but pity on those whose job it is to condemn it without ever having tasted it.

Maanan brought it, and showed us how to light it and to smoke it, one of us dragging at a time. You must know there is at least this much that could frighten uncertain men away from wee, even if the lies about it were not so plentiful. Wee can make you see things that you might perhaps not really want to see. It is not a question of nonexistent things being conjured up. Wee is not magic. It is just that all through life we protect ourselves in so many ways from so many hurtful truths just by managing to be a little blind here, a bit shortsighted there, and by squinting against the incoming light all the time. That is what the prudent call life. The destructive thing wee does is to lift the blindness and to let you see the whole of your life laid out in front of you. Now what you see, whether it comes up from hidden things inside your soul or from the common facts of the waking life you lead, is not false. But its truth is the deep, dangerous kind of truth that can certainly frighten you into a desperate, gloomy act if the life you have been living is already of itself deeply gloomy and deeply desperate. That is the only sensible reason for fearing the thing. I have sat in courtrooms and heard young men sent to waste five and seven years of their lives in jail, and the judges have flatulated through their mouths for hours, yet no one has said any of this at all: that is because they want to protect the weakened and the victimized from the knowledge of what is happening to them. But judges will never know.

We followed Maanan as if she had been our mother, Kofi Billy and myself. She walked with us to the breakwater a little

70

distance from where the market gutter opens into the sea, and we sat there and smoked. Kofi Billy, always looking quietly at the place where his lost leg should have been, was like a child, asking Sister Maanan all the time to tell him what really was going to happen. Maanan only kept passing the burning wee from mouth to mouth and with a smile in her voice told us both to wait till we could tell ourselves the truth. And then all of life changed in a moment. In the first flash I was sure I was about to vomit, but the fear went down and I saw it was the total newness of the feeling. For a moment things outside of me did not press in on me any more. They could not. I was too busy becoming aware for the first time of what my own body was about. I think it was in my fingertips I felt it first: blood rhythm moving in the tip itself, felt for the first time and recognized. I looked and was amazed to see that the fingertips were not visible as thousands and thousands of little fluid bubbles in motion, but as a calm exterior of skin covering bone. And if a fingertip could be so many loose bodies in so much motion, what of the whole body when it felt this way? I could hear the beat of my heart. You don't really hear it normally. I breathed out and in, and came to know that I was taking in tastes and sounds with the air. Then, though he had been close all the time, I heard Kofi Billy saying something and I was startled. His voice was not only close to me in body; but since I had thought what he said before he said it, his voice reached me as if it had been my own coming back to me from some strange place. The voice had said, 'I don't like it here.'

So I asked him why and he asked me if the smell had not grown too powerful for Maanan and for me. It had. We were sitting on the breakwater, above the foundation rocks thrown there on the beach by the builders and used by everybody else as a lavatory and as a bathroom. The night air carried the smell of mixed shit strongly into our stomachs and into our blood now. Maanan, still smiling, nodded slightly, and we all got up and climbed down from the breakwater, moving carefully past the rocks so as not to fall in all the filth, and when we came to the water's edge we sat down on the firm wet sand and the air was clean and moist with salt water.

Down at the edge of the salt water we dragged out the last stick of wee Maanan had brought, and took in with bodies newly opened up everything that was going on inside and outside ourselves. The smoke itself inside the mouth had a repeated sharpness that stung the tender skin below the tongue until we had held our breaths and it had all gone deep inside. I looked at the sea flowing toward and over the sand, and I no longer saw dead water hitting land in senseless waves of noise. The water and the sand were alive for me then; the water coming in long, slow movements stretching back into ages so very long ago, and the land always answering the movement, though in our dead moments we do not have eyes to see any of this. Sounds, the mild thunder of the night waves hitting calmer water and the sigh of retreating afterwaves, now joined together with what we saw. The sand looked so beautiful then, so many little individual grains in the light of the night, giving the watcher the childhood feeling of infinite things finally understood, the humiliating feeling of the watcher's nothingness.

I looked at Maanan. The light was not very strong, but I coul see clearly that she was smiling, and the way she looked made me understand that all the time I had never really looked at the woman Maanan. Or I had looked at her with my eyes and seen images, but thought nothing, and that is a dead way of seeing things, I have known since that first evening on the shore. We all knew that Maanan was one of the most beautiful women, but the way it came to me again that night was different from any time before. The beauty, as always, was there in her face and in the line of the body beside me on the beach. But there was a softness in the face that was entirely new to me. It was not a weak, meaningless softness. Rather, it was as if Maanan's face was all I would ever need to look at to know that this was a woman being pushed toward destruction and there was nothing she or I could do about it. She was smiling at me, but in myself I felt accused by a silence that belonged to millions and ages of women all bearing the face and the form of Maanan, and needing no voice at all to tell me I had failed them, I and all the others who have been content to do nothing and to be nothing at all all our lives and through all the ages of their suffering. So much of the past had now been pushed into the present moment at the edge of the salt water. I would have said something to Maanan if the things to say had not been so heavy, but even then I was sure she understood, that she had understood long before I had ever seen enough to ask her forgiveness, and that she had forgiven me as much as it was possible for the suffering to forgive those who only remain to suffer with them and to see their distress.

And then I did not feel so painfully apart from Maanan any more. Her eyes held mine and in response to her look my mind and heart opened themselves up to the pain of deep feeling. Forgive me, Maanan, forgive us all if that is possible these days. I remember we said nothing at all about love, at this time when perhaps something said might have brought travelers back from frightening journeys, we said nothing about love itself. I reached out a searching hand, but in the end I only held with my fingers a handful of fine, beautiful sand, and the beauty of the sand took my gaze away from the troubled beauty of the woman beside me there with Kofi Billy, and that one moment passed, I did not know then how irretrievably.

I know. It is the easy thing to do, to talk now with the sorrow of time past, as if with time I have grown better, and, given back all the moments that have gone to waste, I would find a way to be closer in goodness to those to whom my impotence has brought pain. All this regret is vain, a way to hide from my own dead nature by pushing it into the past. I know. Yet I feel the regret, and that is why it will not leave me alone, least of all these days.

I could not help it as the moist sand dripped through my weakened fingers and joined the shore. Like an animal I knelt down and stretched out my hand to wash the sand away with the farthest coming water of the waves, and then suddenly I felt like taking the salt water into my mouth. It was not only salt I tasted, but a hundred other strong things in the water, and I cleansed my mouth with it and spat it out slowly and did it all again. Something that did not want to die made me touch Maanan softly on the side of her mouth. For a long time my hand rested there and I looked at her and I was lost in despair.

73

She did not cry then. She only turned her head and following her I saw Kofi Billy. He must have been staring out over the ocean all the time, and he did not turn to face us. He looked so far apart, watching the distances beyond in his uninvolved, silent way, and then after a very long time he raised his head, looked around him and finally rested his eyes, looking at the sand under him with eyes that were large and silent even in the little light there was.

'What do you see?'

I do not know why Maanan asked that question. Perhaps it was a habit she had; to make those she taught to smoke come out of their hiding places within themselves. And I do not know whether she meant the question for me, or for Kofi Billy alone, or for both of us, a vague question thrown in the wind. But Kofi Billy understood the question for himself and began to answer.

'I see a long, long way,' he said, 'and it is full of people, so many people going so far into the distance that I see them all like little bubbles joined together. They are going, just going, and I am going with them. I know I would like to be able to come out and see where we are going, but in the very long lines of people I am only one. It is not at all possible to come out and see where we are going. I am just going.'

The last was an exhausted statement. After it nothing came. Kofi Billy was again looking noiselessly past his wood-and-metal leg down to the sand beneath, his large eyes shining in the faint light.

Maanan lifted up her head and asked if the small moon was not strange looking in its mist. Kofi Billy lay on his back on the moist sand, and when we had almost forgotten about the moon, in a calm voice he said, 'Yes, the moon is very beautiful like that.'

There was nothing either of us could say after that. We sat with Kofi Billy, knowing the accident that had broken him was pushing forward from the calm below, but knowing of nothing we could do, and unable to say anything in the hope of calming fears too deep for the outsider to feel. Then after some time Maanan got up.

'Shall we go?' she asked the two of us. I did not have time to say anything. It was Kofi Billy who answered her – an answer full of his own long bafflement.

'Can we go?'

Maanan held Kofi Billy's hand and very painfully he got up and we walked in the yielding sand up past the decayed rocks, sitting backward on the breakwater and swinging our legs over, then dropping the short fall to the other side. There was nothing around me then that was not joined to everything else. On the way back it seemed so natural that the electric poles should all have lines going between and joining them, and the only lonely, unexplainable thing about the place was the figure of a very young girl leaning against a pole, waiting for someone no one could see. As we moved up to her and left her far behind, she looked more like some insect lost in all the vastness of the world around it than like a female learning the beginning pangs of love. And so we went back; the three of us, the broken man, myself, and the woman, and when we saw again the people we had left to go to the beach that evening it was plain that after what had passed through our minds as we watched the sea we could no longer look at them and hide our knowledge of everyone's despair from them.

There was not much talk after that, not between the three of us, for Kofi Billy hid himself from the world, and said nothing, in fact was not to be seen at all, and Maanan, Maanan was trying after happiness again, in those ways that were to destroy her so utterly in the end. And with the others there was not as much to say as there had been in the past, since more than ever now each man's troubles were just an echo of another man's trouble, another woman's pain.

It was the Sunday after that that Kofi Billy's body was found. He was hanging from a sheet, down from the top bar of the finished door of a house not yet finished then. The leg of wood and metal that he had was covered with his blood, so that it seemed he had made some strenuous effort just before he died, perhaps while he was trying to kick over a large upended brick underneath him. He had not been a violent man ever in his life, though he was so big and we all knew how much he loved to work on something with his strength. But we never really know. It is possible that here was a lot of violence, too much of it, turned finally inward to destroy the man who could not bear it. I would not know how to live with the knowledge of what had happened to him, and the certainty that I would never have the power to do anything about it.

Every one of us was uneasy after this death, because we knew there was no reason he should go alone like that, killing his own self. Each one of us must have thought of it: he was surely not the only one to go, only the first, surely. Voices, when people spoke now, were a little loud and jovial for no reason anyone could see, except perhaps the ridiculous hope that false happiness would reassure the desperate. Even the women were becoming mean. In the market there was nothing they wanted to give, and they were careful about money in a way that brought the sickness home to all of us. We blamed them, as we blamed ourselves and every other thing that was there to be blamed. What can people do when there remains only so much meaning in their lives and that little meaning is running so irretrievably away with every day that goes? What can people do? We were defending ourselves against our friends as if they were animals. Many things happened then which we ourselves had no way of understanding. Strangers, our own people who had gone as seamen to the West Indies, came back wearing only calico and their beards, talking openly of the white man's cruelty. We all said they were mad, of course, but if you stood with one of them long enough and listened to his words without too much fear, toward the end it would become very hard for you to tell on which point exactly the man was mad. And so people feared them, not only for the wild, unaccustomed gentleness of the way they looked, but also for the disturbing, violent truth of some of the things they were so often saying.

Someone else I knew, Tricky Mensah who lived near the harbor, also went on a voyage in a passing ship. He was not away so long, but when he came he had of a sudden turned painfully good, so sadly humble in what he did, singing low hymns and telling constantly of the coming of black Americans

76

with love and power and goods, coming to free us. Does the name Egya Akon say anything to you now? He was a happy man, accepting everybody's jokes against himself, and at a time when money was something no one had, it was said that because he did not drink or smoke, and did not run after other people's women, he was sure to have a lot of money somewhere. He was found dead, killed in his room by men for whom he seemed to have opened the door himself, and those who believe these things will tell you that at his wake his wounds bled clearly when certain of his friends came past; but Egya Akon was a solitary man, and there was no one to make anything but gossip out of what was so openly said. But that was not the end. It was whispered of Slim Tano that he was certainly the man who had got Egya Akon to open his door so early in the morning, because the man loved him and would do anything for him at whatever time it was he wanted that thing done. Egya Akon left no one to do anything to Slim Tano, but Slim Tano by his own self went mad, went completely mad, and the only thing he said that made any sense to people was what he shouted out every ten minutes or so:

'I didn't do it ooooo, I swear upon my father's foot I didn't do it ooooo!'

It was not true that Egya Akon had ever had much money. He did not earn much, and he was a man of this country but he did not have the character to steal from his work. That was why people who could have liked him like a good brother, always ended up calling him a fool. A few pounds, maybe, and that was all his killers could have found. But a few pounds then were not things to disappoint men desperate with the disease of the time. We were all discovering something that seemed hard only when it was new. Money was not pieces of paper the farmers burned to show their wealth. Money was life.

I know it is like a lie for me to talk like this, remembering only these things that were so hard. But the times were hard, and after all what we remember most strongly is what is true for us. I know. There were calmer things, many of them when you think back and bring them up from down below, things that were sometimes good, sometimes beautiful. Wee, which we

77

smoked many, many times more, whenever we could get our own, or whenever Maanan in her descent came up long enough to be really with us for a while and brought some with her. It was not always by the sea, but often enough it was, so that when the time came and we had nowhere to sleep it was nothing new for us to lie on the beach and watch the dawn sky change every morning, with the sweet after feeling of what we had been smoking in the night in us. There was also something in it, though it is hard to say it now, when we sat and passed the single stick from mouth to mouth and joked about the time it took to arrive from the last mouth and the amount of smoke drawn into waiting lungs. There was something there which I know we have lost these days. There was no one there at the time who did not think of himself as something tough, and the times were pushing everyone to become something much like animals, and yet there was something there which made people refuse to go just like that, and when they got something good, they remembered you in spite of everything. It was a desperate time, still, and it was not only Kofi Billy who thought of hiding forever from an alien world impossible to hold. We all, one day or the next, as we went with our hands in our pockets along the empty way from the harbor to the Employment Office knowing we would find nothing but others like us waiting for nothing, as we passed in the night by the water's edge under the faint yellow lights, we all must have thought of things far beyond this place and the time, far beyond life itself. I do not know why we did not all go.

*

There is something powerful that has burned him. The naked body is a covering for a soul once almost destroyed, now full of fear for itself, and full of a killing anguish at what this fear makes impossible. But the man has never really known the thing that turned his friend into a human being hiding from other human beings. Intimations of beliefs held with too great passion and sincerity in the past, of many heavy things seen with a clarity that destroys a person's peace, and that is all. This naked body has an outward calmness about it, but inside

78

it how much power is lying hidden from the watching eye, how much of the terrible energy of a human being fired with strong belief? Something comes out at times, and then it is quickly drawn in again. The man remembers times when his friend has been drawn to speak of something outside himself, and the things he believed were no longer so well hidden, and he had talked in the way he had, that parted everything so clearly into the light and the shadow, the greatly beautiful things that could be and the starkly ugly things that are, so many true pictures given to the listening mind with words, bringing understanding where none had been before. But what a painful kind of understanding, so that he wastes it all in the end with other words that destroy the pictures, words that mix the beauty with the ugliness, words making the darkness twin with the light, and in the end he says what he now believes, that in the end that is the one remaining truth. The man wonders, sitting there, whether this resignation does not make his naked friend infinitely smaller than he could be. Why should there be such a need for shrinking the hoping self, and why must so much despair be so calmly embraced? Is so much protection necessary for life itself? Once the man had asked his friend about this his calmness and his despair, wondering why Teacher should remain so unwilling to move closer to those of his old friends who were now in power. Surely, something could still be done by a good man.

First, Teacher had asked the man, 'Something for which people?' But he had not waited for an answer. 'The things people want, I do not have to give. And no one wants what I happen to have. It's only words, after all.'

The man had said something earnest about the connectedness of words and the freedom of enslaved men, but then Teacher had said one of the harshest things he had ever said. With a shrug he had said that men were all free to do what they chose to do, and would laugh with hate at the bringer of unwanted light if what they knew they needed was the dark. He had told a story he said had meant more to him in his unhappiness than any other story, something he called the myth of Plato's cave. It was not the last time the man was to hear it from his friend, for it possessed a special power over the teller's mind: a story of impenetrable darknesses and chains within a deep and cavernous hole, holding people who for ages had seen nothing outside the darkness of their own shadowy forms and had no way of believing there could be anything else. And out of these, one unfortunate human being is able at last to break from the chains and to wander outward from the eternal circle of the lightless cave, and to see the blinding beauty of all the lights and the colors of the world outside. With the eagerness of the first bringer the wanderer returns into the cave and into its eternal darkness, and in there he shares what he has, the ideas and the words and the images of the light and the colors of the world outside, knowing surely that those he had left behind would certainly want the snapping of the ancient chains and the incredible first seeing of the light and the colors of the world beyond the eternal cave. But to those inside the eternal cave he came as someone driven ill with the breaking of eternal boundaries, and the truth he sought to tell was nothing but the proof of his long delusion, and the words he had to give were the pitiful cries of a madman lost in the mazes of a mind pushed too far out and away from the everlasting way of darkness and reassuring chains.

After each telling of the story the teller would ask, as if he had been speaking to the air, why men should stand apart and disappoint themselves when people free to choose, choose what they want?

*

It is not true at all that when men are desperate they will raise their arms and welcome just anybody who comes talking of their salvation. If it had been so, we would have been following the first men who came offering words and hidden plans to heal our souls. But we did not run out eager to follow anyone. In our boredom we went out to the open public places to see what it was people were talking about, whether it was a thing we could go to with our hopes, or just another passing show like so many we had seen and so many we are seeing now. How long will Africa be cursed with its leaders? There were men dying from the loss of hope, and others were finding gaudy ways to enjoy power they did not have. We were ready here for big and beautiful things, but what we had was our own black men hugging new paunches scrambling to ask the white man to welcome them onto our backs. These men who were to lead us out of our despair, they came like men already grown fat and cynical with the eating of centuries of power they had never struggled for, old before they had even been born into power, and ready only for the grave. They were lawyers before, something growing greasy on the troubles of people who worked the land, but now they were out to be our saviors. Their brothers and their friends were merchants eating what was left in the teeth of the white men with their companies. They too came to speak to us of salvation. Our masters were the white men and we were coming to know this, and the knowledge was filling us with fear first and then with anger. And they who would be our leaders, they also had the white men for their masters, and they also feared the masters, but after the fear what was at the bottom of their beings was not the hate and the anger we knew in our despair. What they felt was love. What they felt for their white masters and our white masters was gratitude and faith. And they had come to us at last, to lead us and to guide us to promised tomorrows.

There is something so terrible in watching a black man trying at all points to be the dark ghost of a European, and that was what we were seeing in those days. Men who had risen to lead the hungry came in clothes they might have been hoping to use at Governors' Balls on the birthday of the white people's queen, carrying cuff links that shone insultingly in the faces of men who had stolen pennies from their friends. They came late and spoke to their servants in the legal English they had spent their lives struggling to imitate, talking of constitutions and offering us unseen ghosts of words and paper held holy by Europeans, and they asked us to be faithful and to trust in them. They spoke to us in the knowledge that they were our magicians, people with some secret power behind them. They were not able in the end to understand the people's unbelief. How could they understand that even those who have not been anywhere know that the black man who has spent his life fleeing from himself into whiteness has no power if the white master gives him none? How were these leaders to know that while they were climbing up to shit in their people's faces, their people had seen their arseholes and drawn away in disgusted laughter? We knew then, and we know now, that the only real power a black man can have will come from black people. We knew also that we were the people to whom these oily men were looking for their support. Only they did not know this. In their minds it was some great favor they were doing us, coming to speak to us in words designed not to tell us anything about ourselves, but to press into our minds the weight of things coming from above. They came hours late when we had been standing in the sun waiting to hear what they had to say, and they came with nothing but borrowed words they themselves had not finished understanding, and men felt like sleepers awakened only to hear an idiot's drooling tale.

'Ah, contrey, so these fat yessir-men in jokers' suits, they are the people going to lead us?'

'Aaah, contrey *broke oo*, contrey *no broke oo*, we *dey* inside.'

A few of the most desperate tried to see what they could do, thinking they would break if nothing was done. The yessir-men gave them gallons of the killing *akpeteshie* and the usual corned beef and gave them things to do to frighten white men. When the desperate men were caught, the lawyers did not even care to look their way. How could they, when all they wanted to do was to show the white master how reasonable, how faithful, how unlike the *akpeteshie* drinkers they were, and how deserving to have power over their people shared with them? So there were the meetings at which people were promised the unfolding of mysterious plans to bring the sorrows of a people to an end. And to the waiters in the rain the end of the expected message was always this, 'Have faith in us. We know the white man and his ways. Have faith in us. Plan R. Plan X. Plan Z.' Better to go home and not go standing in the sun ever again. Better to let the clowns talk to each other and the white men they love with so much fire. All curiosity about the old men who wanted to be new leaders died, and men thought once again of new ways to make despair bearable, and those who could enjoyed it.

The old lawyers and their rallies gave us one good thing to make our days less heavy, something we could laugh at. Afterward it became our habit to sit, anywhere, and watch someone imitate the speech and the English gestures of the men who wanted to lead us. There was one young man who could make every stomach ache with laughter. You do not know him. He had to run away after the last strike at Takoradi. You see, he had seen too many things that were becoming funny about the new Party people. In those days he used to tell us with a very serious expression that he had heard some important news. Then he would act out what he had to say. First, he was the governor getting ready to see his servants, taking up a helmet with feathers taller than himself and marching under it. Then, when the governor sat down, this joker Etse would pause to play another part. Like a penitent thief he would come smiling up to the governor's seat and stammer, 'Massa, I have some news for you, sah.' (African leader's smile.) Turning quickly and sitting down as the governor, Etse would ask, 'Yes, what is it, boy?'

'Sah,' our leader would say, 'mah contrey people no happy, sah.'

'What! After everything we've done for them?'

'Yessah.'

'The ungrateful devils!'

'Yessah.'

'Now, boy, tell me. What is it they want?'

The leadership smile expands. 'Massa, if you make me head man, mah contrey people go happy again.' Wider. Bow. Look of affection and gratitude.

It would be wrong if I talked of those days as days full of unhappiness and nothing else. I wonder in what strange countries Etse is roaming now, driven away by something he loved at first.

We were laughing at some impersonation of his, one empty afternoon, when after a long absence Maanan came dressed to make a man faint and telling us nothing about where she had been. All she would say was that she had come to be at the rally. We knew there was to be a rally at Asamansudo, but we had stopped going long before, and Maanan surprised us all. Etse stopped and looked at her the way a teacher looks at a child.

'Now could you tell us, Maanan, why you should come and insult us like this, leaving full men here to go and listen to the eunuch lawyers?' But Maanan only laughed, so I also spoke.

'Stay here. These old baboons can never give you the things we can give you right here. They have lost all theirs, trying to be white.'

Maanan laughed like a happy woman, and when she calmed down she said, 'You people are late. You haven't seen him yet.'

'Who?'

'The new one.'

'A new old lawyer, wanting to be white.' Etse was not often angry.

'No. He is new, and he is young.' I asked Maanan where he had come from. 'I don't know yet.'

'Is he a stranger then?'

'He is one of us all right. Only nobody knows much about him. They say he does not go talking about himself. Only the work we have to do.'

'He is another fool, then,' Etse said, 'just like the others, talking to men without jobs about the work we have to do.'

Maanan did not even answer him. She looked at us with this strange look of happiness in her and said, 'Come and hear him. Four sharp.' And she went out with the happy light dancing in her eyes, leaving us all wondering what had happened to her at last. And since we had nothing really to do, our reluctance went away bit by bit, and we roamed around the market area as if we had no desire to go anywhere, but at four we also were in the crowd at Asamansudo, and we were quite amazed to see how many people had come. News had been traveling over our heads and beneath our feet, and only now had it come to us.

*

The man has long known of the pain of disappointment inside his friend. In his own way he too had felt it, and it was pathetic that in the past and even now all he had to soothe out the injury would be Teacher's remembered words. But now his friend himself was in need of soothing words. He who had so often helped with his patient talk of the cycle of life and death, youth and age, newness and decay, of the good food we eat and the smelly shit it turns into with time: in spite of all the outer calm, he too was in pain. How often had he not said it – that this was the way with all of life, that there was nothing anywhere that could keep the promise and the fragrance of its youth forever, that everything grows old, that the teeth that once were white would certainly grow to be encrusted with green and yellow muck, and then drop off leaving a mouth wholly impotent, strong only with rot, decay, putrescence, with the smell of approaching death. Yet out of the decay and the dung there is always a new flowering. Perhaps it helps to know that. Perhaps it clears the suffering brain, though down in the heart and within the guts below, the ache and the sinking fear are never soothed. The promise was so beautiful. Even those who were too young to understand it all knew that at last something good was being born. It was there. We were not deceived about that. How could such a thing turn so completely into this other thing? Could there have been no other way? The beauty was in the waking of the powerless. Is it always to be true that it is impossible to have things strong and at the same time beautiful? The famished men need not stay famished. But to gorge themselves in this heartbreaking way, consuming, utterly destroying the common promise in their greed, was that ever necessary? How often had Teacher tried to help by saying it was only life, that every little while it was good to bury the hopes of days impossible to call back, to say that nothing in life has changed, nothing save your own hopes and the pattern of your own disappointments; to say that people are the same, children, young people, old people; to go out and look at them, and wake from dreams with which you torment yourself. To look, to accept, to free yourself to see clearly what can be done and what you most surely cannot do. The listener has heard.

He is not so far in the cave that he cannot hear what is said. But what can a person do with things that continue unsatisfied inside? Is their stifled cry not also life?

*

The new man must have begun to speak only moments before we arrived at Asamansudo, because his voice was still low. He was not making any attempt to shout, and the quietness of his sound compelled us all to listen more attentively.

'. . . serving our own selves . . .' The murmur of the crowd had not died down yet. '. . . not waiting till the white man tells us what jobs to do. . . .' Phrases floating in the breeze, calmly, and the crowd listening. 'Can we ourselves think of nothing that needs to be done? Why idle then . . .?' Words about eyes needing to be opened and the world to be looked at. 'Then we can think. . . . Then we will act.' There was power in the voice that time, a power quickly retracted, and replaced by the low, calm voice.

'We do not serve ourselves if we remain like insects, fascinated by the white people's power. Let us look inward. What are we? What have we? Can we work for ourselves? To strengthen ourselves?'

I stood there staring like a believer at the man, and when he stopped I was ashamed and looked around to see if anybody had been watching me. They were all listening. The one up there was rather helpless-looking, with a slight, famished body. So from where had he got his strength that enabled him to speak with such confidence to us, and we waiting patiently for more to come? Here was something more potent than mere words. These dipped inside the listener, making him go with the one who spoke.

'. . . in the end, we are our own enslavers first. Only we can free ourselves. Today, when we say it, it is a promise, not yet a fact. . . . Freedom! . . .' The whole crowd shouted. I shouted, and this time I was not ashamed.

Near the end, he spoke about himself. If he could have remained that way! But now he is up there, above the world, a savior with his own worshipers, not a man with equals in life.

Then, when he spoke, his words made him look even smaller, even weaker than he had looked at first.

'I have come to you. And you can see that I have nothing in my hands. A few here know where I live. Not much is there. And even what is there is not my own. It is the kindness of a woman, one of you now here. Before she saw me I did what we all do, and I slept on other people's verandas. It is the truth, so why should I feel ashamed when proud men look down and say "veranda boy"? I am not ashamed of poverty. There is nothing shameful in it. But slavery. . . . How long. . . .

'Alone, I am nothing. I have nothing. We have power. But we will never know it; we will never see it work. Unless we choose to come together to make it work. Let us come together. . . . Let us. . . . We. . . . We. . . . We. . . . Freedom. . . . Freeeeeeeedom!'

I was not the only silent one when we met again that evening. Even Etse could find nothing to joke about, though the threat that everything was turning serious was killing him inside. Maanan came much later, and found us all so quiet. We could see her happiness in the movement of her body itself, and it was beautiful. She was a woman in love then.

'Maanan is wetting her womanhood over this new man.' It was Etse.

'Ah, man, let me wet it.' It was surprising that Maanan could be so very happy and yet continue to speak so calmly. 'Let it soak itself in love. Today things have gone inside me, and they have brought out what I have hidden in me. He brought them up. They were not new to me. Only I have never seen anything to go and fish them up like that. He was reading me. I know he was speaking of me. To you too. But did you hear him? How can a man born of a woman tell me my thoughts even before I myself know them? I ask you, how can he?'

'Another wife gone,' said Etse. 'Poor me!'

Maanan was laughing softly. 'And so helpless he looks. He needs a woman to look after him.'

'Preferably Maanan,' said Etse with a sharp quickness.

'Preferably Maanan,' said Maanan slowly, tasting the words. 'Preferably Maanan.'

How could this have grown rotten with such obscene haste? Sometimes I think I will understand it, when I see it as one frightened man's light from his own death. For he was not afraid of the old ones, the jokers. They could not have come and buried him. It was his own youth that destroyed him with the powerful ghost of its promise. Had he followed the path traced out by his youth and kept to it, what would have prevented a younger man, one more like himself in the purity of his youth, from coming before him as more fit to keep to the path? A youth who could have lived the way he himself had lived at first, the way he never could have lived again when he became the old man and shiny things began to pull the tired body toward rest and toward decay. But that would have meant another kind of death for him, this death of which he had begun to walk in daily fear. And so his own end had also to be the end of all that he had begun, and if another promise comes it cannot be the continuation of the promise he held out but which he himself consumed, utterly destroyed. Perhaps it is too cruel of us to ask that those approaching the end of the cycle should accept without fear the going and the coming of life and death.

Or maybe even this is searching too far away. It is possible that it is only power itself, any kind of power, that cannot speak to the powerless. It is so simple. He was good when he had to speak to us, and liked to be with us. When that ended, everything was gone. Now all we do is sit and wait, like before he came. It must be power. I say this because he is not the only one whom power has lost. It has happened to those around him, those who were not always there for the simple sake of the power they could find. Consider your friend Koomson, who will make you rich. Remember me.

Koomson we all have known for a long time here. A rail-wayman, then a docker at the harbor. Pulling ropes. Blistered hands, toughened, callused hands. A seaman's voice. Big, rough man, a man of the docks well liked by men of the docks. Doing well, the only way we do well here. Not spitting at any contreyman, only the fat merchants and their lawyer brothers and Lebanese gangster friends, and that is quite all right here. I still do not know how Koomson got to Accra. Everybody says with a wave of the hand, 'Oh, you know, the ideological thing. Winneba.' True. That is where the shit of the country is going nowadays, believing nothing, but saying they believe everything that needs to be believed, so long as the big jobs and the big money follow. Men who know nothing about politics have grown hot with ideology, thinking of the money that will come. The civil servant who hates socialism is there, singing hosanna. The poet is there, serving power and waiting to fill his coming paunch with crumbs. He will no doubt jump to go and fit his tongue into new arses when new men spring up to shit on us. Everybody who wants speed goes there, and the only thing demanded of them is that they be good at fawning. Is that the place that changed the dock worker Koomson? Or did he go there after he had changed? Because he had changed? I have seen the place, and I have seen him there, and in Accra. He lives in a way that is far more painful to see than the way the white men have always lived here. Is it true then, that after all the talk that is possible, this is the only thing men are looking for? There is no difference then. No difference at all between the white men and their apes, the lawyers and the merchants, and now the apes of the apes, our Party men. And after their reign is over, there will be no difference ever. All new men will be like the old. Is that then the whole truth? Bungalows, white with a wounding whiteness. Cars, long and heavy, with drivers in white men's uniforms waiting ages in the sun. Women, so horribly young, fucked and changed like pants, asking only for blouses and perfume from diplomatic bags and wigs of human hair scraped from which decayed white woman's corpse? Whiskey smuggled in specially for the men who make the laws. Cigarettes to make those who have never traveled cry with shame. How can Koomson return to us? What has he got to say to those he used to work with? Will he come down to see the bodies he left behind and not say a word? Can he sit down with men and smoke wee and curse stupid magistrates for jailing men who have harmed no one? He has come here often, but only like a white man or a lawyer now. Swinging time at the Atlantic-Caprice. Young juicy vaginas waiting for him in some hired place paid for by the government. Important people must relax on weekends. The week is filled with so much killing work. Speeches to prepare. On moral uplift. Socialism. Revolution. Dedication. Interviews to give. The role of the old man in the emancipation of everybody else. So why should he not speak only to the fat lawyers and the fatter politicians? What would we have to say to him? Or he to us? It may be terrible to think that this was what all the speeches, all the hope, all the love of the first days was for. It is terrible, but it is not a lie. Who can blame them when in this society there is no way of knowing whether anything else is possible? If they found the only way they could escape from us, mount far above us, was by first talking to us like brothers, who are the fools? There was something so good about the destroyed people waking up and wanting to make themselves whole again. There was so much that was heart-filling about the friendships and the hopes of the first days. So it should be easy to take the rot of the promise. It should be easy now to see there have never been people to save anybody but themselves, never in the past, never now, and there will never be any saviors if each will not save himself. No saviors. Only the hungry and the fed. Deceivers all. Only for that is life the perfect length. Everyone will tell you, pointing, that only the impotent refuse. Only those who are too weak to possess see anything wrong with the possessing fashion. Condemnation, coming from those who have never had, comes with a pathetic sound. Better get it all first, then if you still want to condemn, go ahead. But remember, getting takes the whole of life.

CHAPTER SEVEN

The naked man stood up on the bed and tried to reach over to the door and take down a pair of trousers hanging on a nail behind it, but at his touch the door swung left and away from him, and he had to jump down and go round to get the trousers. He slipped them on over his naked body and took down a T-shirt from another nail. As he put it on the man on the desk watched him closely, wondering how a man like him could see so clearly through the rot and yet find the strength to live in it, against it. The man remembered times when Teacher had talked with eagerness about hopeful things, but then always there was the ending, when he would deliberately ask whether the rot and weakness were not after all the eternal curse of Africa itself, against which people could do nothing that would last. Sometimes this death of hope would spread all over the world. When Teacher had talked of people standing up and deciding then and there to do what ages and millions had called impossible, had talked of the Chinese Mao and the Cuban Castro struggling in the face of all reasonable hope, even then Teacher's mind would look beyond the clear awakening and see after the dawn the bright morning and the noonday, the afternoon, dusk, and then another night of darkness and fatigue. Once he had asked whether it was true that we were merely asleep, and not just dead, never to aspire any more. So even after the big movements he hopes for, the question always remains with Teacher: it is all worthwhile, then? And he sighs from long habit, reproaching himself for wishing after impossible dreams.

'I have to go back now,' said the man.

'I know. I'll go a little way with you.'

As his friend locked his door behind him, the man said, 'You know, Teacher, I feel really tired these days. I don't think I work any harder. But there is not so much desire.'

91

'No. Maybe you're working for something else, now.'

'I am not sure.'

'Well, first of all, you work for yourself.'

'Myself?' asked the man. 'I'm not at all sure. I know I would not be doing the things I do now if I were by myself.'

'Ah, yes,' said his friend. 'The self immersed in your loved ones is a very different self from the self alone.'

And there is no hope anywhere of breaking loose.'

'No. It is exhausting, this chasing after gods not of our own making.'

'You used to see some hope, Teacher.'

'That was such a long time ago.'

'Not so long a time. Six years?'

'But in my mind the time is buried under centuries now. True, I used to see a lot of hope. I saw men tear down the veils behind which the truth had been hidden. But then the same men, when they have power in their hands at last, began to find the veils useful. They made many more. Life has not changed. Only some people have been growing, becoming different, that is all. After a youth spent fighting the white man, why should not the president discover as he grows older that his real desire has been to be like the white governor himself, to live above all blackness in the big old slave castle? And the men around him, why not? What stops them sending their loved children to kindergartens in Europe? And if the little men around the big men can send their children to new international schools, why not? That is all anyone here ever struggles for: to be nearer the white man. All the shouting against the white men was not hate. It was love. Twisted, but love all the same. Just look around you and you will see it even now. Especially now.'

'I have looked, Teacher,' said the man. 'I only wish I could speak with your contempt for what goes on. But I do not know whether it is envy that makes me hate what I see. I am not even sure that I hate it, Teacher.'

'It should depend on what a person wants himself, no?'

'But, Teacher, what can I want? How can I look at Oyo and say I hate long shiny cars? How can I come back to the children and despise international schools? And then Koomson

92

comes, and the family sees Jesus Christ in him. How can I ever feel like a human being?'

'Yes. Life gets very hard when veranda boys are building palaces in a matter of months. If you come near people here they will ask you, what about you? Where is your house? Where have you left your car? What do you bring in your hands for the loved ones? Nothing? Then let us keep quiet and not get close to people. People will make you very sad that you do not have a house to make onlookers stumble with looking, or a car to make every walker know that a big man and his concubine have just passed. Let us keep quiet and watch.'

The rain had not been much, and it had made scarcely any noise, but outside, the little gutters by the roadside had swift little streams in them now, rushing toward the sea, and the air was misty, as if the rainwater had not fallen, but remained suspended, gathering heaviness.

'Teacher,' said the man, 'you know it is impossible for me to watch the things that go on and say nothing. I have my family. I am in the middle.'

'Will you let yourself be destroyed first, then?'

'I don't know. When I speak of Koomson my wife looks at the children and I can see how sorry she feels for herself.'

'You will have to leave her to enjoy her own sorrow. Unless you are eager to destroy yourself to feed her desires. O you brave married men. In the end you have to see the redness of her gums. If it frightens you, you don't get married at all. You run away like a coward, like me. But you are brave. You have chosen to fight her. And the whole society is behind her.'

'It's been a very soft rain,' the man said after a pause.

'Yes,' his friend said. Then, 'I am sorry I have been unable to give you what you need.'

'What is that?'

'Strength, I suppose.'

The man laughed weakly. 'Don't worry,' he said. 'You know what you're about. And you understand. That's enough for me'

'You are kind,' said the other. I know my life is empty, one thing yours is not. Now all I do is read books of other places

93

and other times, listen to the music of South Africa and the Congo and the Afro-Americans. And often I remember Maanan and the bitterness and the emptiness of life rise up in me. That is all.'

Near the place of the prostitutes there were little puddles left by the gentle rain, some beginning to flow, looking for gutters. Occasionally the naked bulbs of street lamps shed a little light on holes in the back walls of bathrooms filled with strands from communal sponges cemented with the green moss and old suds killed with dirt and sweat so long ago, and the water still trickling out.

'You have come a long way, Teacher,' said the man.

'I will leave you here then.' The two shook hands and the man stood looking as his friend walked back, his steps quickening in the empty night. From a distance he called back, 'Please don't forget to give your wife my love.' The man laughed with a low sound and made no reply. He stuck his hands once more deep into his pockets and walked evenly in the direction of the breakwater and the sea.

At the breakwater he turned right for the long walk back. His head felt unusually light, but every few moments there was a sharp pain in the neck where the spine was. Inside himself the man felt a vague but intense desire, something that seemed to be pushing him into contact, any kind of contact, with anything that could give it.

In the past such moments had always come with thoughts of life and the usefulness of living persons, when it was possible to look again at everything that went on and to think that perhaps even this was the best there could be. Having the whiteness of stolen bungalows and the shine of stolen cars flowing past him, he could think of reasons, of the probability that without the belittling power of things like these we would all continue to sit underneath old trees and weave palm wine dreams of beauty and happiness in our amazed heads. And so the gleam of all this property would have the power to make us work harder, would come between ourselves and our desires for rest, so that through wanting the things our own souls crave we would end up moving a whole people forward. At such times the man was

94

ready to embrace envy itself as a force, a terrible force out of which something good might be born, and he could see, around close corners in the labyrinths of his mind, new lives for Oyo; for the children with their averted eyes; for himself also. Then in the morning the thick words staring stupidly out from the newspapers, about hard work and honesty and integrity, words written by men caring nothing at all about what they wrote, all this would come to mean something.

But then in the office it is hard not to see that even this little peace of mind is an illusion. Hard work. As if any amount of hard work could ever at this rate bring the self and the loved ones closer to the gleam. How much hard work before a month's pay would last till the end of the month? Rent going up and up. In the man's area the landlord is the uncle of the rent control man, and both call themselves Party activists. One man had tried to get his rent reduced, wiring to the Party Secretary in Accra. Poor fool, he still believed. He was called a saboteur, a nation wrecker, and many other Party words, and then in the end, since he would not stop his talk of justice, he was taken by the police to Accra. And food. How long would it take, and how hard the work, before there would be enough food for five, and something left over for chasing after the gleam? Only one way. There would always be only one way for the young to reach the gleam. Cutting corners, eating the fruits of fraud. The timber merchant and his piled-up teeth, offering the bribe, the way. Once when the man was traveling to Cape Coast three different policemen had stopped the little bus and asked the driver for his quarter license. The driver had not bought it yet, and each of the policemen had said to him, in front of everybody, 'Even *kola* gives pleasure in the chewing.' In each case the driver had smiled and given the law twenty-five pesewas, and the law was satisfied. There was only one way.

Zacharias Lagos, living so long here that he had forgotten he was ever a Nigerian. Working for a sawmill, and getting, in the days of pounds and shillings, ten pounds twelve a month. But Zacharias lived like a rich man. Every evening a company truck brought home great lengths of healthy wood which

95

Zacharias in his wisdom had written off, and he sold all of it. When he was caught people called him a good, generous man, and cursed the jealous man who had informed on him.

Abednego Yamoah, still free, perhaps never to be caught. Selling government petrol for himself, but so cleverly there is always someone else, a messenger, a cleaner, to be jailed, never Abednego. The whole world says he is a good man, and the whole world asks why we are not like him.

That has always been the way the gleam is approached: in one bold, corrupt leap that gives the leaper the power to laugh with contempt at those of us who still plod on the daily round, stupid, honest, dull, poor, despised, afraid. We shall never arrive. Unless of course, we too take the jump.

And there are many, so many, pushing us to the edge and praying that we jump any terrible how and also get close to the gleam, dragging them after us. The loved ones would be the first to curse fate if the would-be leaper landed in prison. The loved ones are also the first to look with longing at the prosperous leapers and everything the leap has got them. Revolving thoughts of speed, of Oyo and cars and drivers, and of accidents. Cowards only are afraid to drive. And Koomson has learned to drive. So the loved ones are in the lead when we are stripped of the little self-respect that remains at this age. The chichidodo. Nothing is left. We dwindle into nothing at all, with nowhere to stand.

The pain, whatever one might wish to say, is truly unbearable when you see some twin of yours shoot like a star toward the gleam, so fast that he has light of his own to give. And at five in the early morning you get ready to walk obscurely into your little hole to start the morning shift in the ghost world of the unsuccessful and the cowards, waiting with eyes that begin to burn with who knows what is wrong, waiting for the senior men to come in anytime after nine. When will even that be reached? There is no call to worry yourself now. It will be reached when you are so old you cannot taste any of it, and when you finally get to it it will not be a reward. It will be nothing but an obscene joke.

The rain had stopped a long time ago. On the road, only the

noise of unseen puddles stepped in and the reflected light of lone cars in the night gave any indication of the wetness of everything. Nearer home there were sticky pools of mud even in the middle of the road, and the man had to be careful, watching every step and squinting to get a guiding reflection from the ground before moving.

He scraped the mud from off his sandals on the little veranda, and when he went to the door he found there was no need to knock; it was only closed, not locked. He pushed it gently open and entered. The air that hit his face and pushed its way down his nostrils was hot, and for a moment he had a desire to go back outside, but after a while the heat became a noticeable but comforting warmth, and the man began to think it had been very cold outside. He switched on the light and saw that the hall was empty. His wife and all the children were inside, then. From the table near the door he took a key and went out.

When he opened the kitchen door he saw that everything had been made ready for the coming dawn. There was water in the bucket, in case, as happened so often, the tap was dry early in the morning. The coal pot was full, and there was even a wad of paper stuffed into the hole under it, and beside the bottle of kerosene was the box of matches. Good. The man locked the kitchen door and returned to the hall. He locked that door also, took off his still wet sandals and put them on the floor near the door, and, without turning on the bedroom light or switching off the one in the hall, he went in.

On the floor the bodies of the children lay carelessly caught up in the hanging folds of their large mosquito net. The man did not disturb them, but went directly through the door of the wooden screen, pulling the curtain across after himself. He took the clock at the head of the bed and turned the knob to set the alarm. It had been turned already. The man put down the clock, took off his clothes, and, wrapping himself with his cloth, stepped out into the hall and put out the light. In the darkness he closed his eyes for a few seconds, opened them, and without any difficulty found his place inside the screened-off area, on the bed beside his wife. In the darkness he had the illusion that the form beside him could belong to a stranger, an unknown woman, and the illusion filled him with a strong, unusual desire. His eyes were finding the darkness easier, and he could see the dark outline of his wife's body. Still, there was nothing unpleasantly familiar about it. The cloth covering it had slipped onto the bed beside the sleeping woman, and she was quite naked.

The man put out his hand and touched the body in between the thighs, just below the genitals. The flesh yielded too readily, and the dreaded sense of familiarity threatened to return. The hand moved up. The vagina itself was harder, more resisting, almost abrasive in the sharpness of its hair and the dryness of outer skin. Wanting the satisfying moistness of a woman aroused at last, the man pushed his hand farther up and then bent it, searching for the hidden knob of flesh. But the movement had brought his wrist against his wife's belly, and the long line of a scar took the man's mind completely away from any thought of joy.

The last child had had to be dragged out of its mother's womb, and when she left the hospital the long scar was still only a sore underneath all those bandages. The sight of the scar never ceased to provoke an involuntary shudder in the mind, running down the spine and stopping only at its base. Now, as usual, the touch itself filled the tired mind with traces of blood and the color of flesh newly exposed, and the tortured face of a woman alone, then Oyo's forgiving eyes in the hospital afterward, when he had gone to visit her. There was love in her. There had always been, of course, since he had never had anything else he could have given her. If now it could not come out, perhaps the fault was not with the woman herself. Perhaps the fault was with the soul born without the luck of other souls? No. With the mind unable to decide to do what everyone was saying was the necessary thing, what everyone was doing.

Thinking he has awakened his wife, the man turns toward her, preparing a smile. But she is asleep. He props his head in his palm, leaning on an elbow, and the thoughts of the scar he has not learned to live with are driven out by the strong smell of a woman unprepared for love, and he moves his hand away from his head. In the world of uncertainty before real sleep the man sees himself as he is, but pushed back into time already done, having to go back to school and sit through all the old examinations and tests. The half-dream is not new, and again the man is overwhelmed by his own inadequacy. In the examination hall he finds all movement impossible, so that he cannot even tell if he knows any answers.

CHAPTER EIGHT

Blinding lights, wild and uncontrolled, succeeded by pure darkness, from which the recognized self emerges. The man sees himself, very small, very sharp, very clear. Walking with an unknown companion, scarcely even seen, in the coolness of some sweet dusk, leaving the dark, low hovels behind. Out in the distance, far away but very clearly visible, a group of shining white towers, having the stamp of the university tower at Legon and the sheer white side of the Atlantic-Caprice. They are going there, the two of them, the man and his companion, happy in the present and happy in the image of the future in the present.

But brutal lights shine and cut into the night with their sudden power, rushing with their harsh rhythm toward the happy pair, now so confused. The lights move forward, smooth and powerful. The man, blinded by a cutting beam, covers his downcast eyes with his hands, and in the movement lets go of his companion's waist. But she is not blinded. Through the insufficient protection of his fingers he can see her, her eyes shining with the potent brightness of huge car lights, returning the power of the oncoming lights. They come, the lights, with the noise of the cars bringing them. Sound, hardly audible, of a new door opening. Floating upward in the air, the man's companion lands inside the car in the lead. The other cars, a procession of gleaming cars reminding the watcher of long lines of OAU men in American vehicles, swing up behind the first, and all of them go off in the direction of the towers, leaving the man behind. The white towers gleam with a supernatural radiance as the cars get closer to them, then everything penetrates slowly, smoothly into darkness as they enter. Every shining thing goes out when only the man is left, and the darkness turns keenly cold. Looking for warmth, he lies down, but the ground is also cold and very hard. The man tries to find his way back

100

into the old warmth of the hovels he has left behind, but looking back, he finds he can never again know the way back there.
All he can feel now is the cold, and a loneliness that corrodes
his heart with its despair, with the knowledge that he has lost
his happy companion forever, and he cannot ever live alone.

Before the clock's alarm could ring, the man's hand reached
out and smothered it. He had been half awake for some time,
and the chill before the awakening had yet to leave him. These
days it was as if there were an inner system, alerting him with
his own anxiety, making him wake even without the mechan-
ical help of the clock. Deep in the back of his mouth something
irritated the roof and he strained to get it out. Three hard, small
stones which he squeezed between thumb and forefinger. The
smell of the little pits never ceased to amaze and to disgust him
with its unbelievable potency. From the head of the bed he
took the large towel and wrapped his body in it. So early in the
morning there would be no one up, and no need to rush to take
the bathroom. In car-tire sandals the man walked out, over to
the bathroom, and satisfied himself that the flow of water from
the shower there had not been cut off in the night. He took his
soap dish with the sponge in it and decided to endure the cold
water. It would be better not to wait till the others got up.

*

When the man had switched on the light within the bathroom
and shut the door, he could not for a time take his eyes off the
door where it was rotten at the bottom, and the smell of dead
wood filled his nostrils and caressed the cavity of his mouth.
He tried to breathe in only small, saving breaths of air, but
when the cold water hit his back he sucked in a huge involuntary gulp, and there was no more point in his continuing
his efforts to keep the rot out of himself. While he soaped
himself he felt the growl of his bowels, and in a momentary
panic he wondered if it would be necessary for him to use the
home latrine. But the rumble subsided, and he knew he could
wait till he got to the office. A terrible preference.

Under his feet the cement floor was covered with some sort
of growth. It was not the usual slippery bathroom growth. In

101

fact, it was not really visible at all, and yet to the soles it felt quite thick, almost comfortable if one forgot to think about it. The hole leading the water out was again partly blocked with everybody's sponge strands, so that the scum formed a kind of bar just before the hole and the water underneath went out very slowly, a little at a time, and there was a lot of it covering the floor when the shower had been running even a little while. The man threw the sponge he had been chewing into his soap dish, turned up his head and rinsed his mouth with the falling water. Then he washed away the soap from his body and quickly dried himself, taking care not to have his towel touch the smelly wood at the bottom of the door or the covered, soft floor under his feet. When he had finished, he stepped into his rubber sandals and went back to his room.

While powdering his crotch and putting vaseline in his hair, the man searched in the table drawer and found some change, enough for the day's fares and even for some lunch, perhaps. He felt there was more there, but there was no need to look and see how much there was in all. In his underwear he went into the kitchen and brought the cold water in the kettle and mixed himself a drink from the remaining Ovaltine. His wife had not told the entire truth to the intruding woman beggar the night before. There was some sugar left, though not so much that it could be given away. She was right. Drinking his cold Ovaltine and eating the cabin biscuits he turned on the radio, letting the red line roam until he got his favorite music, the sounds from the Congo. He could hear his wife moving about inside, certainly awake by now, but probably not wishing to come to him there in the hall, listening for indications that he had left. If he left early enough, he could of course catch the dawn train from Kojokrom to the station and save himself the fare. If he left early and walked fast enough to make the long distance to the emergency stop. He went in, not looking at his wife, took his trousers and shirt, making sure this time to take also a handkerchief, and went into the hall again to dress. How many other days had passed without his saying anything to the children?

The walk over to the stop was always longer than he thought

102

he could remember. When he arrived, he did not have to wait too long before the slow train came, and for a moment he thought it would pass him by, but it stopped almost reluctantly. There were others, about five in all, waiting for the train, but no one had spoken and when they were inside the silence remained unbroken all the way to the station. Everyone alone with his troubles. Better.

At the station, getting down from the train the man slipped on a patch of slime near the entrance. Looking down he saw the mess of some traveler's vomit. Though not fresh, it had not had the time to get completely dry. He went around it and descended carefully onto the concrete of the station platform, then walked down the long stretch of it toward the entrance of the Block. From the shadows two lean figures emerged as if to threaten him, but when he came up to them they saluted stiffly and said 'Mornin', sah.' Two men from far away, lost in the mazes of the south. He thought of saying he was not a 'sah,' but the idea itself was so ridiculous when you came face to face with men calling you sah. What could men like the two have found down here, if anything? What kind of misery was here that they could not have found at home? Or could it be the same escape for them also? Possible. It is possible that far away somewhere, young men sigh in the night and dream of following these, but they certainly do not know the end of the journey. Quiet, anyway. These may be envied men, not to be pitied, not to be wept for by people uncertain of themselves. On the way, other night figures are encountered, like the latrine man just coming round the corner from the downstairs lavatory, the junior men's latrine. There is not much light, but not much light is needed to tell one that the man with the shitpan heavy on his head has an unaccustomed look of deep, angry menace on his face, and his eyes are full of drunken fury. Perhaps the smell of *akpeteshie* would be bathing him if he were not carrying this much stronger stench with him. Surely that is the only way for a man to survive, carrying other people's excrement; the only way must be to kill the self while the unavoidable is being done, and who will wish to wake again? It is not such a usual thing to see the shitman coming at

103

this hour of the morning. The shitman is a man of the night and the very early morning, a man hidden completely from the sight of all but curious children and men with something heavy on their minds in the darkness of the night. And it is not such a usual thing to see a latrine man up close.

The last shall be the first. Indeed, it is even so.

Already. Up the dark stairway of the Block, the man searches for and finds the switch for the light above the stairs, turns it, and continues the climb. When he comes up to the office door he sees the watchman coming up the stairs two at a time, his keys rattling with a curiously unmetallic, dull sound in his hand. The man searches for the railwayman's pass in his pocket, but the watchman indicates he recognizes him, and holds the door open for him. Then, for no reason the man is aware of, the watchman says, 'Thank you, massa.'

Massa. Strange word. Strange name.

Inside, he turns on all the lights. The moist, hot scent of closed-in Ronuk is thick in the room, and the man goes to the windows and opens each of them as far as it will go, bringing in a little of the morning air. Then he turns and walks to his table under the big rail chart and raps the dead Morse machine before switching it alive. Warning raps for contacting stations up the line, but at the first three there appears to be no one to give an answer, and he stops. It is not time yet, anyway, though it should be very soon now. He pulls out a drawer, looking for something to fill time with. There are four pencils in there, government violet, all very blunt, and a piece of a blade by them. He takes them, goes over to one of the waste boxes, slides it all the way across the floor to his desk with his foot, and sits down to sharpen the dead pencils. Before he has finished sharpening the third of the pencils the door opens, and at first he assumes it is another cleaner entering in the morning, but the new arrival walks straight past his desk and says good morning. The man returns the greeting of the space allocations clerk, resisting the temptation to ask him why he has come so early just this day. Maybe there will be an explanation offered, though this space allocations man is not known for too much talking. Nothing is offered, and curiosity wins.

104

'You've come early today,' the man calls out to the clerk.

'The early birds ...' – long pause – 'catches the what-you-call-it, so to speak.'

No use asking for any explanation of this strangeness. Perhaps another man running away from loved ones at home, so early in the morning. The man sits watching in his puzzlement. The clerk goes to his cage. There is the sound of drawers being pulled out, papers being moved about. When the clerk comes out of the cage he walks to a window on the street side and just stands there, looking out and down.

Staring at the chart in front of him, the man hears a very audible rumble from somewhere inside him. It is followed immediately by a terrible pulling pain in his abdomen, and he thinks there is a saving plug in his anus which threatens to drop out at any moment now. There is an upstairs lavatory, but it is not open. Only the Senior Service men have keys to it. No matter. Even the one downstairs is better than the one at home. Taking some old, stiff paper from a drawer, he hurries downstairs, making an effort to hold his buttocks together.

For some reason the lights in the latrine are brighter than anywhere else, making the cement platforms stand up like old monuments. The man leaps up on the cleanest he can find, near the far end of the long latrine, passing his eyes over the row of cans encrusted with old shit. When he chooses the one he will use he is careful, in letting down his trousers, not to let the cuffs fall into the urine grooves in front. The thing that makes this place better than home is that here there is air, even if this air also rises from the holes below and is misty with the presence of familiar particles suspended in it. Squatting up there, he lets the air from below blow a cooling draft against his buttocks, and he looks at the crowded wall opposite, with the ceiling the wall is still a dazzling white where there are no webs to hide the paint. The color does not really change until about the level of the adult anus. There the wall is thickly streaked with an organic brown, each smear seeking to avoid older smears, until the dabs have gone all round the wall. There are places where, it seems, men have bent down to find an unused spot to use, and in a few incredible places men seemed to have jumped

105

quite high and then to have accomplished a downward stroke. There must have been people who did not just forget to bring their paper, but who also did not bother to drop their loads, for the wall has marks that are not mere afterpieces, but large chunks of various shit. The man's eyes seek refuge above the brown, at shoulder level. No brown smears here, only occasional scribblings in pencil, mostly the government color. A small drawing of sex in an impossible Indian position, with the careful lettering:

VAGINA SWEET

But just to the right of this there is something the man has seen before without noticing its companion:

MONEY SWEET PASS ALL

To the left there are others, a bit harder to make out at first.

WHO BORN FOOL

SOCIALISM CHOP MAKE I CHOP

CONTREY BROKE

The man feels the last of his innards come down and when he has finished enjoying the relief it gives him, he wipes his bottom, pulls up his trousers and jumps down, buttoning up on his way out. Near the door the large challenge assaults him again:

YOU BROKE NOT SO?

That, and the two companion statements following, make him smile.

PRAY FOR DETENTION

JAILMAN CHOP FREE

On the climb up the man feels his nostrils assailed by something he is carrying with himself, the smell of the latrine. He turns back down the stairway, deciding to go for a clearing walk in the street outside. There are only a few sellers out now, and none seem to have come for the morning. Perhaps only those who have fallen asleep in the dawn, to wake up later and go home to sleep a little more, if there are any homes. Behind him a figure, round and short, enters the Block. Perhaps a worker he had not recognized. The man walks absently in the direction of the bus stop on the hill, and only when he comes to the end of the UTC building does he stop again to ask himself where he is going. Nowhere. It is getting lighter, too. He walks back past the shops, through the entrance and up the stairs.

When he opens the office door there is loud, pleased laughter inside, and a voice with a vague familiarity says, 'No. This is only your *kola*. Take it as *kola*.' Another laugh. 'I was sure you would understand, if only I could find you properly. My friend, if you get the logs moving for me, I will see you again. Don't worry. I will take you to my own house.'

'It's all right,' the allocations clerk kept saying. 'It's all right.'

When he got to his desk the man looked more closely and saw the timber man with the many rows of teeth, this time in a suit that made him look like someone's forgotten bundle. He was happy.

'Hey, my friend,' said the timber merchant, 'get my card. Get my card.'

The clerk reached out and took the proffered card, saying, 'Thanks.'

'Ho ho, don't thank me. I am the one to thank you. Ho ho ho!'

The timber merchant turned to go out. As he passed by the man's desk and saw him he stopped as if he could not believe he had actually been in the same room with him all this time. Then he burst into harsh, hostile laughter.

'Ei, so you are here today too. Contrey, why you try to do me so? You don't want me to eat, contrey? Okay. Take yourself. I get man who understands. Ei, my friend, why you want to play me wicked?'

The man said nothing, but the timber merchant still stood in front of him, staring at him as if he expected an answer to his question. The man turned to look at his chart to see if there would be any answer to his Morse signals now. Behind him the timber man laughed again, very shrilly, and shouted at him, 'You. You are a very wicked man. You will never prosper. *Da.*'

The man said nothing, did not even look back at the hurler of the insult. There was an answering signal on the machine,

107

and he listened to it, not bothering to write down the letters. It said 'Prestea.' Someone else just testing in the morning. The man gave a further answering rap, and tried another station farther up the line. To his left there was the sound of the door closing behind the angry timber man.

'What did you do to him?' It was the voice of the allocations clerk.

'I told him I could do nothing for him.'

'I see.'

'Will you bring his timber?'

'Yes. He has learned his lesson.'

'What lesson?' asked the man.

The clerk answered with a chuckle, nothing else. It is so normal, all of this, that the point of holding out against it escapes the unsettled mind. Everyone you ask will say the timber merchant is right, the allocations clerk is right, and you are a fool, and everyone is right the way things are and the way they will continue to be. The foolish ones are those who cannot live life the way it is lived by all around them, those who will stand by the flowing river and disapprove of the current. There is no other way, and the refusal to take the leap will help absolutely no one at any time.

The Morse machine rattles wildly and the signature says it is Obuasi. Again. Better answer him as if nothing were wrong.

'Morning.'

'You are there.'

'Yes.'

'Say why.'

'Work.'

'Say why.'

'Wife.'

'Say why.'

'Be serious.'

'Goway. Say why.'

'Children.'

A very long pause, then a long rattle. At first the man thinks it is all without meaning, but when he writes down the individual letters what he gets is an endless 'Hahahahahahahaaaaa.' To the maniac he taps a reply. 'You mad.' Another long laughing roll, abruptly cut short.

'Yourself.' Silence. Nothing more to say, then, 'Mines train loading.'

'Start time.'

'0619. Fourteen m late.'

'Fine.' The man thinks of slipping in his question.

'Who be you?'

'Your father hahahahaha.'

'Mad you hohohoho.' From the other end, only silence now.

The office fills up as the day clerks enter, first the small boys and messengers, then the other clerks. About nine-thirty the Senior Service men come in each with his bit of leftover British craziness. This one has long white hose, that one colonial white white. Another has spent two months on what he still calls a study tour of Britain, and ever since has worn, in all the heat of Ghana, waistcoats and coats. He would have made a good Obedient Boy of the Empire on a Queen's Birthday. When the Supervisor of Space Allocations enters, the allocation clerk hurries to his office. The two of them know each other well, and owe each other a lot. It is well known that the supervisor was once, before coming to the Railway Administration, a bursar at one of the Ghana national secondary schools. As is the custom in this country, he had regarded his job as an opportunity he had won for making as much money as he could as quickly as he could, and his handling of the school's finances had soon made his intentions clear. The students had complained to the Ministry of Education. The Ministry, as is usual in this country, had searched for the students most responsible for the drafting of the letter of complaint, and dismissed them for gross insubordination. The remaining students had rioted. The Ministry, looking for more students to dismiss, had closed the school down. There had been no financial probe, of course, but none would have been possible, anyway, since a fire had gutted the bursar's entire office during the rioting. Very shortly after that the Railway Administration was advised from above to appoint the bursar to this new job. He had brought the

109

allocations clerk with him, and there was a likelihood that it was he who let it be known that the fire in the bursar's office was not the work of students.

The allocations clerk is in there with his boss for something like half an hour, and when he emerges he is closely followed by the supervisor and they are both smiling broad, very satisfied smiles. Let them smile. This place is kind to them, so let them smile. In another country they would be in jail. Here they are heroes.

Automatically, suppressing his irritation with himself and with all things around him, the man concentrates on the incoming Morse messages, writing them down swiftly and sending back short replies, asking questions, exacting replies. At lunchtime he feels really hungry and goes down to the sellers.

He would like some good *fufu*, but without a lot of meat, street *fufu* is miserable food, and with meat the cost will crucify a man completely. What he can afford there is *gari* and beans with palm oil, and in spite of the worrying thought that it is not called concrete for nothing, the man begins to enjoy it. A poor man must learn to suffer with his bottom also. He takes his pan and moves under the shade of a nim tree, smiling at the loco workers already there. Between lip smacks, the talk is the usual talk, of workers knowing they have been standing on the windy shore with their snuff at their fingertips, never going in. Between sighs and bits of bitter laughter, phrases that are too familiar pepper the air. 'He is only a small boy. ...' 'Yes, it's the CPP that has been so profitable for him. ...' 'Two cars now. ...' 'No, you're way behind. Three. The latest is a white Mercedes. 220 Super.' 'You will think I am lying, but he was my classmate, and now look at me.' 'Ah, life is like that,' 'Ei, and girls!' 'Running to fill his cars. Trips to the Star for weekends in Accra. Booze. Swinging niggers, man.' 'Girls, girls. Fresh little ones still going to Achimota and Holy Child. ...' 'These Holy Child girls!' 'Achimota too!' 'He is cracking them like tiger nuts.' 'Contrey, you would do the same. ...' 'True ... money swine.' 'Money swine.'

In a group the workers move off to wash their hands. The

110

man waits for them to finish, then goes in his turn to the tap and cleans the oil off his hands. Then he goes up and sits again at his desk. True, concrete indeed. It is impossible to resist the drowsy feeling. There is a little time yet, so he slides his chair over to the right and puts his head down on the desk to sleep. A voice laughs and shouts something about Passion Week, but the man is already slipping into sleep and he does not care that much anyway.

When he wakes up it is past two, and his place at the desk is already occupied by the new boy. The boy sees him and gets off the stool he has been using.

'Sit down,' the man says, 'sit down. You're very early.'

'Yes. I had nothing to do. Also, I wanted to watch, and try.' The eagerness of the innocent. He will one day wish he had never seen the Block. He will one day wish he had never been born, but not yet.

'Would you mind if I took over from you now?' The question startles the man, so that he does not answer at once. 'I want to perfect my Morse.' In the front of his head the man feels a persistent pain, rising and falling with the beat of his heart, and the thought of an afternoon off gives him a huge feeling of relief.

'Are you really sure you want to?'

'I have nothing to do.'

'Fine. Anything I need to tell you?'

'The chart is clear. No, nothing.'

'Thanks.'

Sometimes a certain type of relief comes like that. You reach the latrine just at the point when you think you will have to let go in another moment, anywhere. And then, there are times like this when relief is not expected, but when it comes no one has to tell you that it is what you have been needing all along. The man goes down the stairs, and this time he has not the energy to keep his hand off the dirt-caked banister, and he lets it slide greasily down. The pain in his head goes and comes, goes and comes. When he gets to the street he turns left immediately and walks along the side of the road, keeping out of the way of the afternoon harbor traffic.

After the level crossing there is the harbor gate, and the man there does not let him pass at once but takes his card and stares long at it, then with an air of extreme but defeated reluctance he motions to the man to pass. He walks a long way under the cool shadow of the new overhead conveyor, and when he comes to the end of it he goes around the terminal warehouse and sits down at the edge of the wharf with his legs dangling over the water.

One always wonders why the sea is not much dirtier than it turns out to be. In the afternoon sun it is very calm. Even the motion of it is quiet, ending by adding to the general sense of stillness. There is a feeling like the one that comes when one rides on the back of a motorcycle, or moves in any open way at a great speed. Thoughts of the past and the present, hopes and fears for the future, all come with the speed of the vehicle, and at the end a man is quite exhausted, having gone again into parts of himself not often visited. The thoughts rising from the sea all have a painful hopelessness, so the man rises himself and goes walking along the edge of the wharf, making for other docks. A harried man comes into sight, balancing himself on a raft of timber logs packed together on the water, calling out the names of timber laborers around him, also standing on floating logs, and marking everything down on a tally sheet pinned to a board in his left hand. He shouts a lot, and in the afternoon sun the veins on his neck glisten with sweat. Farther along, a small ship, looking very old with the red and black paint on it, flying a flag the man has never noticed in this harbor, is being filled with cocoa in brown sacks. The driver of the long truck on which the bags are piled sings a plaintive song, and the sound, coming from such a man, surprises the listener completely. The singer has taken off his shirt, and the back that lies exposed is brown and muscular. Kofi Billy used to love this kind of work. Up on the little ship there is a knot of black bodies waiting to direct the coming load, and now and then faint sounds of many people's laughter come curling over the side from the hold below. In the small rooms above the deck itself two white men in white shirts and white shorts, one of them very short, stand looking downward at all the men below, at all the shouting and the labor below. The man leaves the ship behind and walks out in the direction of the main breakwater swinging out into the ocean. The sounds of violent work grow fainter as the wind rises past him, and keeping to the edge where he can see quite far down into the sea, he walks without any hurry, not having to think about time or going back, feeling almost happy in his suspended loneliness, until he comes to a flight of stairs built into the side of the breakwater, leading down into the sea. He leans over and looks at the steps. They descend in a simple line all the way down, dipping into the sea until they are no longer visible from above. The man sits down, and, feeling now a slight pain at the back of his neck, throws back his head. Small clouds, very white, hold themselves, very far away, against a sky that is a pale, weak blue, and when the man looks down again into the sea the water of it looks green and deep. A sea gull, flying low, makes a single hoarse noise that disappears into the afternoon, and the white bird itself flies off in the direction of the harbor and its inaudible noise, beautiful and light on its wings.

CHAPTER NINE

On a Sunday morning the habit of a whole week does not die of itself. The accustomed mind is ready to do the necessary things it does not want to do. It is only with an effort that the promise of rest enters the tired body.

Before dawn his own inner anxiety had awakened the man. He had not taken care to cover himself properly with his cloth in the night, or perhaps it had slipped off him while he slept. His back felt keenly cold. Another day. But with wider awakening the last night's preparations came back to him. There had been none of the daily necessity to store water, to get the coal pot ready and to have the sponge and the towel waiting with the bucket near the door. And the little clock would not go off after all. Without looking at the form lying beside him, the man turned in order to free the cloth from under his body, held it out at its full length, and wrapped himself completely in it, covering his head. Then in the comforting darkness he had created around himself, he went back to sleep, all anxiety gone.

There was strong daylight inside, even in the bedroom itself, when he awoke. He did not have to get up yet, but lay thinking of the things he had done the day before. He had exchanged time off and gone down High Street, shopping for the special food and drink his wife had decided to feed Koomson and his wife with. It had been impossible, of course, to find any of the really expensive drinks his wife would have wanted, like the British White Horse whisky and Vat 69. She always wanted these drinks when there was an important person to be entertained. Once she had told him why, and her reason was that any ruffian could buy and drink beer. True enough, though even that was getting less and less true, with the rise in the prices of things.

The day before, going into the shops with his new money in his pocket, he had had the uncontrollable feeling of happiness and power, even while knowing somewhere in the back of his

114

mind that the expensive things he was buying would deepen the agony of his next Passion Week. When he had asked for all that white man's food, the beautiful long rice in the packet with the Afro-American Uncle Ben smiling on it, the tinned cake which had traveled thousands of miles from rich people's countries, and the New Zealand butter, he had known it was stupid to be feeling so good just because he was buying these things he could not in the end afford, yet he could not help the smile that came to his lips and spread this feeling of well-being over all his body. If the aristocratic drinks, the White Horse whisky and the Vat 69, had been available then, he would have bought them gladly in the foolish happiness of the moment, no matter how bitterly he would have cursed himself later. It was not only because of the admiring glances of people in the shops, for whom a man's value could only be as high as the cost of the things he could buy. And it was not all of it because of Oyo's words, her happiness when an important visitor could praise what he had been given, and her angry silences when there was nothing but the food of ruffians and the drink of ruffians to be given to these big people when they came. There was also, inside the man himself, a very strong happiness whenever he found himself able, no matter for how brief a spell, to do the heroic things that were expected all the time, even if in the end it was only himself he was killing. How was it possible for a man to control himself, when the admiration of the world, the pride of his family and his own secret happiness, at least for the moment, all demanded that he lose control of himself and behave like someone he was not and would never be? Money. Power.

When all the call of sleep was gone from his body, and the man got up and put on his khaki shorts and went out into the hall, he found his wife standing in front of the meat safe, staring in a lost way at the food in it and at the bottles of beer in front of it. The man went and stood beside her, resting a light arm on her shoulder.

'Did I leave out anything?' he asked.

'The food is fine,' she said. 'The food is fine, but the drinks . . .'

115

'There was only beer in the shops,' he said.

'Yes, in the shops.'

'And you don't like the made-in-Ghana spirits.'

The woman put her hand to her throat in a swift movement of disgust, then smiled. 'No,' she said, 'I don't like made-in-Ghana spirits. But there are good drinks in the country still.'

'Only in the homes of big shots and Party socialists.'

'They must get them from somewhere. They try, that's all.' She was quiet for a moment, then she said, 'You must know people who could get you these things. After all, people don't go to school for nothing.'

The man turned his wife around so he could look at her directly, then with a slow fury in his voice he said, 'If any of my classmates are busy smuggling European drinks into this country, they have not told me.' The woman seemed not to have noticed the anger in the man's answer.

'You know that is not what I meant,' she said. 'Things get done all the time, and if you know the people who can do these things, there is nothing wrong in that.'

'I don't know people who can import anything specially for me.'

'Some people do.'

'Besides,' said the man, 'there is nothing wrong with beer.' His wife looked at him in such a way that he could not mistake her contempt. 'After all, Koomson knows we are not rich, so why should we pretend?'

'Are we pretending if we just try to give them the best?'

'Maybe we should wait till we have the money,' he said apologetically.

'Maybe we won't live that long.' When she said that she laughed, a single short sound, and then she bent down and took out the rice and the canned food from the meat safe and walked into the kitchen with it. Then she came back and opened the bottom drawer and brought out all the special plates and bowls and glasses; and she could not suppress a smile as she looked at them. The man helped her take them into the kitchen. They were covered with dust and the droppings of cockroaches and geckos, as they always were after

116

long periods when they had no important visitors coming to eat with them. From the top drawer the woman took out large towels, white and pink, and went to hang them out in the sun to get rid of the must.

The man began to haul the bulky armchairs out into the open. Every time he cleaned them, he wondered why they had to be made so heavy. He could think of only two good reasons: it would take a long time before they needed to be repaired or actually thrown away, and also it would be very hard for any thief to carry them away. Two good reasons why every poor young man furnished his room with these town hall chairs. Still, there was so much unnecessary heaviness and ugliness.

He opened the glass front of the bookcase and took out books he had not looked at in a long time. They were mostly books from his school days, textbooks for the School Certificate Exams. Looking inside some of those books now, he wondered whether he could pass those examinations over again if he had to. At first he had had no doubts at all, after his results came and he knew he had got a Grade II Certificate. He had felt quite confident that in a few years he could take the advanced levels. Then he would have left the Railway Administration, which had been for him at that time only a temporary stop, and he would have gone over to the University at Legon. Not long after he had started work, he had gone there to see a friend, one of his seniors at school. The University was very new at the time, in fact only half finished, but the white beauty of the place had left in his heart a certain long ache ever since he had begun to understand that he could not enter that other life. Another path was open before him. He would have liked to think that he had not chosen that path, that the daily life of a struggling railway man was merely something that had been forced on his unwilling soul. But in truth he could never believe this of himself. Oyo's pregnancy had not pleased him, but he could remember clearly now that the anguish he had expressed when her parents had come with their long story of their daughter ruined had not been entirely genuine. And the marriage ceremonies had actually left him feeling quite happy, with the sense that something important had happened to him.

Now, of course, it looked as if the important thing was simply that he had cut himself off from the future, that he had chosen to make the dry struggles of the present stretch out and consume the whole of his life to come.

He took the books outside, and when he returned he saw that at the back of the case there was a small family of mice, the little bodies lying one on top of the other in soft, helpless confusion. With a broom he swept the mice out and put them, still alive, into the rubbish box outside. The children, sitting around the *oware* they had dug in the ground, turned to see what there was, then lost interest and continued their game.

Inside, the man took the cushions one by one from the floor where he had dropped them, and looked at the material of which they had been made. There were hundreds of tiny holes in the pattern of the cloth. It would be necessary to buy new covers soon. It would be necessary to buy new cushions, in fact, but of course that was altogether out of the question. He took the cushions out and piled them up on one of the armchairs, went back in, and began to sweep the hall, first bringing down the dust from the window sills and from the tops of the remaining furniture. When he had swept the floor, he mixed the remaining bit of polish with kerosene and went all over the exposed floor around the edges of the linoleum with it. After every such cleaning he could not help being disappointed. The place looked so much the same, the linoleum still looked beaten, with the color gone in too many places, leaving only black patches that nothing at all could hide; the red of the polish had nothing new, nothing encouraging about it – it was tired and menstrual. The dark browns of the furniture managed to leave only an impression of great age and dullness. By the time he had finished cleaning the hall, the man was no longer battling with the weight of the feeling that it was all senseless anyhow, all this work which never changed the hall from its depressing self. Something else would be needed for these desired changes, something that he could not hope to have. It would be the same for the children. They would grow up accustomed to senseless cycles, to cleaning work that left everything the same, to efforts that could only end up placing

118

them at other people's starting points, to the damning knowledge that the race would always be won by men on stilts, and they had not even been given crutches to help them. Perhaps one of them would one day break free from the horrible cycle of the powerless. Perhaps one of them would grow up and soar upward with so much power that there would be enough left over to pull the others also up. Dreams. Dreams to break the backs of children with. Dreams to give a moment's peace to the parent who knows inside himself that things never work out that way.

The sweat was coming out freely from his body. When he had done the hall, he wiped the polish and the kerosene from his hands, using a leftover bit of the old drawers he had torn up for a rag. Then he switched on the wireless set. He had left it on Radio Ghana, and now he got the record choices in Akan. He sat down in one of the empty town hall seats outside and listened to the high life sounds coming through the open door. The children out in front of him seemed at the same time to be playing their game and watching him closely. He turned the chair sideways and sat looking away from the children in the direction of the next house. At the end of the record choices, he went back in and turned off the set, took what he needed for a shower and went to the bathroom. He washed himself quickly, holding his breath as long as he could. Then he went back, got dressed in his government khaki trousers and a white shirt, and went into the kitchen.

The children were already eating their lunch, round, single sliced pieces of *kenkey* with each a smear of sardine stew on it. The man took his plate from on top of a little stool, where his wife had placed it.

'I would have brought it to you myself, out there,' she said.

'It doesn't matter,' he said. 'I wanted to eat with you.'

'I have had mine,' she said.

'I don't believe you,' the man said. But the woman only smiled. The man insisted. 'At least you can keep me company.'

The woman began to eat with her husband. The children had moved out of the kitchen itself when their father entered, and

119

sat just outside the door, keeping their eyes away from their parents within. The man could see how little the stew was with which they were trying to eat their *kenkey*. But it had always been like that. Once or twice he had impulsively given up his food so they could have more meat. But if he really wanted to give them the food they needed, they would certainly have to go naked, or he would have to go hungry. The *kenkey* inside his mouth tasted dry, like chaff. He rose before the feeling of hunger had left him, and his wife sat there saying nothing, just staring after him.

'I want to take the beer over and put it in Bentil's fridge,' he called out over his shoulder.

'Ah, good!' his wife said, smiling. 'But can't you wait a bit?'

'What do you want?'

'If you can take the children over to my mother afterward...'

'If your mother can bear the sight of me.'

'My mother doesn't hate you. Not as much as you like to think.'

'I am sure your mother is secretly in love with me, Oyo,' he said.

'Not in love,' she answered. 'Not in love, but she won't bite you.'

He was silent, but inside his head the refrain circled like a stuck record: Only because she has just three teeth left, only because she has just three left.

'Also,' the woman added, 'could you tell Mama to come earlier, about seven?'

'What for?'

'You won't be interested.'

'All right,' he said, 'I'll tell her.'

The children were already waiting. He sat the smallest up on his shoulders, bending his arms to hold her dangling legs. The child held on to his hair as if she feared she would fall down otherwise.

'Hey, Adoley,' the man called.

'Papa.'

120

'Do you want to pull out all my hair?'

The child giggled, still maintaining her desperate hold, then very carefully she let go of her father's hair, holding on to his forehead with her little hands. The oldest child was carrying the bag with the beer in it. The boy had taken two single bottles out of the bag, and he was carrying them very carefully, his face screwed up in unaccustomed concentration as he walked. The eyes of the big girl roamed with an unsettled restlessness over everything along the way. Occasionally she was unable to contain some comment about things she was noticing for the first time, or about people she knew who lived inside the houses they were passing by. The newer houses, middle-type estate houses built by the government for renting, attracted her wonder most. Her comments sounded like words unconnected to anything. They rose and died very quickly, with the passage of the houses, but in the adult mind they left an unpleasant echo that turned the child's every perception into the seed of an accusation that would reveal itself with growth.

'This house belong to Mike.' Whatever happens to the soul of a little African child who grows up thinking of himself as Mike? 'Mike's father has a car.' The girl was swinging the bag a bit and looking up at her father. She has done nothing wrong, to notice that someone's father has a car. It would be quite unreasonable to blame her for what she sees. 'The wireless in the house we just passed is the biggest in the world.'

The boy broke his silence to spell out the word, 'L...i...e ...s!'

'One day you will also see it,' the girl said resignedly. She had lost interest in what was behind her, and she was looking at the other houses coming into sight. Suddenly she gave a sort of sharp cry of delight. 'Ei, look! There is television in that house. The middle one.' She turned in a full circle, swinging the bag. 'Television is so beautiful!'

'B...o...s...s!' the boy spelled.

'Ask Father,' the girl said. 'Papa, is television not very beautiful?'

'Yes, Deede,' the man said. 'Television is very beautiful.'

'You see!' shouted the girl in triumph. The boy bared his

teeth and pushed his head out menacingly toward the girl, but she only laughed. The man's neck was beginning to hurt from the weight of his little daughter.

Down the small hill leading to his mother-in-law's house, they moved more quickly because of the slope, and it was not long before they could see the dead-looking hedge of dry thorn bush surrounding the house they were going to. When the man could see the withered sunflower stalk sticking out behind the hedge, he deliberately slowed down, letting the children go on ahead. He had no desire to have to go inside the house and sit down trading unfelt greetings with his mother-in-law. The girl with the bag was hurrying ahead, and the boy had only begun to make up his mind to chase after her when he stopped in the middle of the street and looked down at his left foot. He was quite near the house now, and he remained bent over, looking at his toes, until his father caught up with him.

'What is it?' he asked.

'Something has cut me,' the boy said.

The man put down the girl he had been carrying and bent down to examine the boy's big toe. It was bleeding a bit now, but there was nothing in the cut, and the man could not decide whether the boy had stepped on a thorn or a piece of broken glass. The bigger girl had disappeared into the house, to emerge a moment later with her grandmother. The old woman's right hand was wet and greasy with oil palm juice, and she held it stiffly away from her body. She kept her gaze trained on one or the other of the children, deliberately avoiding the direct look into the man's face.

'Have you all eaten this morning?' she asked the bigger girl. The girl nodded, but the old woman did not appear altogether satisfied. 'Is that the truth you are speaking, Deede?' The girl nodded once more. The old woman seemed about to interrogate her further, but at that moment she noticed the little boy's limp.

'Ah, my husband!' she shouted, shuffling forward. 'Who is it has hurt your foot? Who did it, my little husband?'

The child whimpered a little and said 'Nobody.' The woman directed an unbelieving glance at the man.

122

'My poor husband!' said the old woman, over and over again. 'You have no shoes to wear, so your poor little feet get torn to pieces. Ei, my husband, you have nobody, nobody to buy you shoes, so your little toes will all be destroyed.' She went close up to the boy and peered down at his feet, looking for the one with the cut on it.

'Where is the wound, my husband? Where is it? You must know you have nobody, you are an orphan, a complete orphan. You mustn't run around, like people who have men behind them, to buy them shoes. My poor husband!'

The man stood quietly, watching and listening, wondering whether he would have any moisture left in his mouth for framing words. This was done so very often, the tender heads of children serving as things on which adults could bounce their bullet words into the hearts of their enemies. He had come to expect it, yet every time it happened it made him angry. With his tongue he freed his teeth from the dry hold of his lips, and spoke to his mother-in-law. His voice had in it the politeness of deliberate effort.

'Oyo asked me ...' he began. The old woman cut him short.

'Ah yes, the suffering daughter of mine, what does she say?'

'Oyo asked me to bring the children along.'

'Oh, I will take them!' she exclaimed dramatically. 'I will take them off the poor woman's hands. My God, how she must be tiring herself! Oh my dear, dear God!'

'Mother,' the man said evenly, 'your daughter is alive and well.'

The old woman peered into the man's eyes, looking up, for she was short. It was as if she were probing intently for some hopeful meaning to what the man had said. Her eyes were very far in, very deep, and they seemed always to float in a small, dry quantity of tears.

'Is that what you say,' she asked at slow length. 'Do you really say my daughter is alive? And is she also well?' The man restrained a smile. 'Ah, then we thank the Lord!'

'She also asked me to tell you to come earlier, about seven.'

123

The old woman's mouth was now set in a very small circle of wrinkled resentment. Without unwrinkling it she managed to tell the man, 'I have heard.'

The man took the two bottles of beer from his son, added them to the others, and took the bag from his older daughter. As he turned to go, he could hear, with a terrible distinctness, the voice of his mother-in-law, assuring his son that he would not grow up to be a useless nobody, that he would be a big man when he grew up. The man walked very quickly until he came to the nearest corner, and it was not until after he had turned that he slowed down and walked relaxedly on, free from the pressure of the old woman's measuring glance on the back of his neck. A short way up, he knocked at the door of a house standing all by itself, went in, gave the bottles of beer to his friend, and walked out again. He felt very free and very light, and walked with slow steps, enjoying his own movement. He walked close to the large incinerator, cutting across the field in the middle of which it stood, breathing in the strong smells of burning animal skin and hair, burning paper and old ash. He did not go all the way onto the main road, but walked along the little street parallel to it, until the two came together at the bridge over the big lagoon.

The strength of the breeze surprised him as he walked over the bridge. When he thought about it, it occurred to him that the reason was just that every time he passed that way there was a lot of traffic on the bridge; and he had never found the time to think of the breeze. Today the bridge was quite deserted, and all the time that he was crossing it there was not even a single car that passed by him. He turned left immediately after the bridge and went away from the sea, walking along the side of the lagoon. The black mud of the small shoreline felt very fine even under his sandals. He kicked aside pieces of old shells lying on the green–black sand, and as he did so a hard gust of wind occasionally lifted off the lagoon, driving forward laden with the promise of rot. A dead fish floated in the water at the edge, the silvery flesh of its belly dancing quite violently up and down with the little waves. When he looked closer he saw a whole lot of little fishes eating the torn white body, breaking

124

the water's surface at dozens of small points. He followed the swing of the road, leaving the lagoon to the left and going by the football park. There would be a game in the evening. There were many hours yet to go, but already small crowds were forming around the gates and beneath the big C.O.S. posters announcing the game.

HASAACAS versus KOTOKO

The swing of the road widened until, just beyond the land wall of the park, it took a definite bend to the right. The man followed it, walking steadily but slowly, and when he got past the Central Prison buildings behind their high wall, he crossed the railway where it cut across the road and headed toward the hills with the bungalows on them. Near the cemetery he saw the same old golf courses that had looked so enormous and forbidding when he had been a child. These fields were still beautiful, especially the green of the grass, which surprised him still with its freshness and its complete cleanness. Five white men and three white women came down the road. Hidden in the group, in stiff white uniform, were two Ghanaian men with prosperous-looking bellies. Four little boys struggled behind them all, carrying their bags and sticks. As they went past, one of the black men laughed in a forced Senior Service way and, smiling into the face of one of the white men, kept saying, 'Jolly good shot, Himmy. Jolly good.'

He was trying to speak like a white man, and the sound that came out of his mouth reminded the listener of a constipated man, straining in his first minute on top of the lavatory seat. The white man grimaced and made a reply in steward boy English: 'Ha, too good eh?' The black men both laughed out loud, and the one who had spoken put both hands to his paunch.

As he got farther into the hills, the man remembered bits of the same old show from the past. Young push-babies with frowning faces broke through hedges behind different kinds of carriages, turning down long, winding roads. Stewards in white uniforms moved swiftly around behind high hedges giving the

125

intruder suspicious glances full of hate. Not everything was entirely the same, though. Here and there the names had changed. True, there were very few black names of black men, but the plates by the roadside had enough names of black men with white souls and names trying mightily to be white. In the forest of white men's names, there were the signs that said almost aloud: here lives a black imitator. MILLS-HAYFORD . . . PLANGE-BANNERMAN . . . ATTOH-WHITE . . . KUNTU-BLANKSON. Others that must have been keeping the white neighbors laughing even harder in their homes. ACROMOND . . . what Ghanaian name could that have been in the beginning, before its Civil Servant owner rushed to civilize it, giving it something like the sound of a master name? GRANTSON . . . more and more incredible they were getting. There was someone calling himself FENTENGSON in this wide world, and also a man called BINFUL.

Another black push-baby passed, pushing a white and pink carriage. But inside the baby was black as coal, and it was stifling in a lot of woolen finery. The man remembered his friend Teacher's bitterness when he thought of all this. So this was the real gain. The only real gain. This was the thing for which poor men had fought and shouted. This was what it had come to: not that the whole thing might be overturned and ended, but that a few black men might be pushed closer to their masters, to eat some of the fat into their bellies too. That had been the entire end of it all.

A feeling of tiredness entered the man's body and he thought of the distance he had already walked. He turned back, trying to quicken his pace.

CHAPTER TEN

The six o'clock news was not yet over when the man got back home. On his way he had heard practically all the news, from other people's radios opened full blast to tell the world outside that here, too, and there, and there, people lived who had a powerful radio. He turned on the set as soon as he entered the hall, and in a few moments he had caught the tail end of the news, all the ritual bits of praise that seemed to be all the news these days. Osagyefo the President bla bla, Osagyefo the President bla bla bla, Osagyefo the President bla bla bla bla. Finally the announcer gave the results of the day's football matches. The man waited until he heard the score that interested him most. Hasaacas one, Kotoko nil. Then he turned off the set. There would be a week of celebration because of this victory, and because of that the coming Passion Week would be severe indeed.

Oyo came out of the kitchen, tired but smiling with pleasure.

'I think you should go and get ready,' she said.

'What about you?'

'I still have a few things to do,' she said. 'Then I can wash and get ready.'

'Can I come and see the things you've done?' He followed her into the kitchen as he said this.

'No,' she laughed. 'Secret.'

Inside the kitchen the man could see only clean basins. The things arranged in them had been covered over with the big towels.

'But if you want to do something,' the woman said, 'you can put the chairs back in the hall.'

The man lifted the chairs and put them inside. When he had the last one in he thought of arranging them in a different pattern, not having them face each other in two pairs with the center table between them. But the other way looked ridiculous in the smallness of the hall, so he gave up and went back to the same old style. By the end he was sweating all over again, and when he went to wash himself the water had a soothing coolness that made him forget about the musty air and the rotten door, and he stayed quite a long time in the bathroom, coming out finally with his body very tired and very relaxed all the way in, even to his bones. He started dressing slowly while his wife was going to the bathroom, so that when she came back he still had only his underwear and shirt on, though he had taken out the trousers he was going to wear and they hung on the dividing screen in the bedroom. The woman put her soap dish down, holding her cloth up around her breasts.

'You are taking a long time,' she said. 'Have you become a leper?'

'Why, are you in a hurry?'

'I just thought you'd get out and let me dress.'

'Ashamed to be seen naked by lecherous strangers, Oyo?'

'Ah, look at it if you want to. It's you who'll lose your appetite for it, not me.' She smiled with the words, but he could sense her old fear in her voice, and he said nothing. She let her cloth fall and he could see her flabby belly with the scar on it. Every time he saw it it looked bigger than he thought it should be. He took down his trousers, pulled them on quickly, took his shoes and socks out with him into the hall, and sat on the hard chair in front of the table to put them on. Afterwards he re-arranged the books in their case and closed the glass front. Oyo came out and went back into the kitchen, holding her iron comb in her hand.

'Jesus!' he said when he saw her, 'you aren't going to do that, are you?'

'I am.' She came out of the kitchen with one of the covered basins, then went back in and in a few moments the man could smell the burning hair. Feeling quite vague inside, he went to her and stood watching the oily smoke pouring out and up from her hair.

'That must be very painful,' he said. Immediately, he was wishing he had not said it.

128

Oyo put the comb back among the coals, then lifted up her head and said, 'Of course it is painful. I'm just trying to straighten it out a bit now, to make it presentable.'

'What is wrong with it natural?'

'It's only bush women who wear their hair natural.'

'I wish you were a bush woman, then,' he said.

She laughed rather bitterly and said, 'You men are hypocrites. You would be angry if we didn't do these new things.'

'Some would.'

'You're all the same,' she said, picking the red-hot comb up from the coals and running it three times through her hair. Then she put the comb aside and washed her hands. 'If I had a wig, there would be no trouble.'

'If you had a wig,' the man muttered, 'I'd be in jail.'

'What do you mean?' she asked sharply.

'Stealing by means of employment.'

'You talk so much of theft.'

'I know it's the national game, but I fear it still,' the man said. His wife laughed, the kind of laugh that answers a very childish statement.

Oyo's mother did not come at seven. At seven-thirty she still had not come, and Oyo asked her husband whether he had really remembered to tell her to come early.

'I told her,' he said, trying to hide a smile.

The old woman arrived shortly before eight, trailing the children with her. They all smelled like freshly washed babies, and their faces and arms were white with talcum powder. The old woman sat down in an armchair, letting out a whole series of sighs that sounded like complaints unspoken. The younger woman got up, but before she could walk out her mother asked her, 'Where are you going, Oyo?'

'I'll give the children something to eat.'

The old woman's mouth contracted with contempt and outrage. 'So you people have been sitting here thinking I was starving your children,' she said.

'Ah no, Mama. I only asked.' The man sat there, watching the two women, saying nothing.

'I fed them!' the old woman went on. 'I fed them and they ate it all, so hungry they have been all their young lives. You really must not let them go hungry like that.'

'Mama,' the younger woman was exasperated, 'we give them enough food. Why do you have to talk like that?'

The old woman withdrew into a sullen silence. Occasionally she sniffed suspiciously and made small disapproving noises in her throat. The man fidgeted in his discomfort, then, making a sudden decision, got up and went into the open air. He had at first only intended to create for himself a moment's respite from the company of the loved ones, but the outside air had a coolness and a friendliness that made him wish he would never have to go back in to all that familial warmth. He made up his mind to wait outside until the Koomsons arrived and he had to go in with them. Walking very slowly so as to consume time, he went in the direction of the house alone by itself, where he had gone earlier in the day with the beer. He found his friend Bentil in and sat down to talk for a while. It was only when his friend said he had to go out to see some old friends that the man realized how late it was – long past nine.

He took the beer, thanked his friend, and started back thinking he would go and find the visitors already in, his wife frantic and her mother stewing in resentment of him. But when he got to the first junction he saw the powerful headlights of a huge car coming straight at him, then turning to the right, going in his direction. He walked faster.

Koomson and his wife Estella were already seated when the man got in. He had found their car parked near the house, with the driver in it, hunched over the wheel. Oyo sat opposite Koomson. Her mother sat next to her, lost in admiration of the Party man's chubby profile. Estella Koomson was in the other chair. The man went up to the visitors and shook hands with them, muttering something about the beer as an excuse for coming so late. Estella Koomson's handshake was limp, and she withdrew her hand in an insulting hurry and wiggled back in the chair, making it quite plain that she was used to softer, more caressing material beneath and behind her. Koomson himself looked obviously larger than the chair he was occu-

130

pying. The man, when he shook hands, was again amazed at the flabby softness of the hand. Ideological hands, the hands of revolutionaries leading their people into bold sacrifices, should these hands not have become even tougher than they were when their owner was hauling loads along the wharf? And yet these were the socialists of Africa, fat, perfumed, soft with the ancestral softness of chiefs who had sold their people and are celestially happy with the fruits of the trade.

The man looked uncertainly into his wife's face. In such situations he felt like a stranger from a country that was very far away, seeing everyone and himself also involved in a slow, sad game that would never end. It was awful, was it not, that the rich should have this effect on the poor, making them always want to apologize for their poverty, and at all times to sacrifice future necessities just so that they could make a brief show of the wealth they could never hope to have.

A smile of secret contentment, flashing from his wife, broke the uncertainty. From one of the covered basins she drew out five shiny glass mugs and placed them, each with its accompanying napkins, next to the chairs. The man took his and placed it next to himself on the table, away from the group. Then he opened the bottles of beer, pouring out the first mug for each person and leaving the half-empty bottles beside them.

'Cheers!' said Koomson. He looked ready to add something as he raised his glass, but the high voice of his wife cut the air to pieces.

'This local beer,' she was saying, 'does not agree with my constitution.'

'And what sort of constitution is it that you have?' asked the man from his isolated place. His mother-in-law took her eyes off Koomson's double chin for just the time required to spray him head to toe with a flaming look. Estella Koomson had not bothered to listen to the question. She contemplated the diamond on her third finger, raised the hand itself, in the manner of a languid white woman in the films, to raise a curl that was obscuring her vision and push it back into the main mass of her wig, and continued as if no human voice had interrupted hers.

131

'Really, the only good drinks are European drinks. These make you ill.'

'As for me,' said the man, raising his mug, 'they do not make me ill. Perhaps in the pocket, but nowhere else.'

His wife and her mother were looking downward in utter humiliation. Koomson made a noise as if to clear his throat, but he had nothing to say, or had not yet thought of anything.

'You should have bought European drinks,' Estella pressed on, 'and not have wasted your money like this.'

'There are none to buy. We tried,' said Oyo sharply.

'Ah,' Estella said with a sigh, 'if you had asked me I would have told Uncle Asford, and he would have brought you some.'

At last Koomson found words. 'It doesn't matter. After all, beer is beer.' He raised his mug dramatically and took a gulp, then exclaimed, imitating the man on the billboards, 'Ah, Star!' When the mug came down it was empty, and a small stream of beer was running down the Party man's lower jaw. Oyo leaned over, took a napkin and wiped it off for him, then poured some beer from her own bottle into his mug.

'Service ... with a smile!' said Koomson, his own face spreading out in idiotic happiness. Soon Oyo was very busy filling up mugs as they got empty. Even Estella eventually reconciled herself to being an African and drank the beer with a sour face. When the drinking had gone on for some time, Oyo asked if everyone was hungry enough to start eating.

'Ah, no, no!' said Koomson happily. 'Wait till I tell you a story.' His wife was frowning, but he was not looking at her. He closed his eyes and began. 'Some people think being a Minister is all good-time. Heh, heh, sometimes I wish I had been a businessman instead. One day they brought a man to give the Ministers and the Parliamentarians and the Party activists a lecture. That was during the Winneba days. The man had many degrees, and he was very boring. In the first place he was dressed like a poor man.' Estella snickered happily. 'And for a long time he spoke to us about economics. They say he was telling us how to make poor countries rich. Something called

132

stages of growth. I have tried to find out what he really said, but it seems I wasn't the only one who slept that day. I woke up when I heard some clapping. The others also woke up, and we all clapped and said "yeaah yeah." Then the Attorney General, who is one of our Party scholars, got up to give the vote of thanks.

' "You have told us, Professor So-and-so, of the stages of growth. We thank you very much for having told us about your speciality." The Attorney General swayed, being drunk as usual, and went on. "Now we shall share our special knowledge here with you. We present . . . the stages of booze!" I tell you, no one was going back to sleep. The Attorney General opened his red eyes from time to time and chanted:

' "Stage One – The Mood Jocose.
Stage Two – The Mood Morose.
Stage Three – The Mood Bellicose.
Stage Four – The Mood Lachrymose.
Stage Five – The Mood Comatose." '

'Then the Attorney General fell down. He was in the final stage himself. We all said "yeaaaah yeah". It was a fine day indeed.'

Oyo and Estella were laughing, Oyo with a bit of a puzzled frown. Koomson was himself shaking with laughter.

'But the funny thing,' he was saying, 'the funny thing was that only the Professor stood there, not laughing even once. I hear he has left this country.'

The old woman asked her daughter to explain the joke, and while she was trying, Koomson spoke once more.

'Request, please,' he said, raising a finger like a schoolboy. 'Nature is calling. Please take me to your toilet.'

From his seat apart, the man suppressed a nervous giggle and said simply, 'We don't have a toilet here.' Oyo looked astonished.

Preening herself, Estella asked, 'So how do you er . . . what do you do?'

The man, enjoying himself now, gave her a long reply. 'We

133

have a place all right,' he said, 'only it isn't anything high class. It isn't a toilet, you see. Just a latrine.'

Koomson exploded into loud laughter. The man saw his mother-in-law's face contract, oozing shame and hate mixed together. Estella had a joyous, condescending smile on her face.

'Well, so long as there is a place. Nature's call is nature's call.'

The man got off his chair. 'Fine,' he said. 'Let's go.' The two men left their women and went off toward the bathroom and the latrine. The cement of the yard was slippery underfoot with a wetness that increased as they got closer to their goal. When they came to the latrine, they found its door locked, and had to wait outside. The agony and the struggle of the man inside were therefore plainly audible to them, long intestinal wrangles leading to protracted anal blasts, punctuated by an all-too-brief interval of pregnant silence. It was a long battle, and the man within took his time. Koomson stood peering into the darkness around the bathroom hole, and though he could see nothing, the atmosphere itself of the place seemed to subdue him. Once the man could hear him swallow very audibly. A man who had escaped, now being brought close to all the things he had leaped beyond. Finally the harsh sound of old dry newspaper being softened in the hands of the man within came at the end of a long, tearing, unambiguous sound and the two relaxed in readiness. Then a small boy emerged.

The boy, in the dark light filtering through from the open doorway of the latrine, appeared still to be wiping his left hand on a piece of leftover newspaper. As he advanced past the waiting pair, a stench came up behind him like a sea wave and hit the men directly in the face. Koomson let a small gasp escape him, hesitated at the door, then, with just a single glance into the entrails of the latrine, he turned back. He said nothing to the man, and the man did not ask him anything. There was no need for words. The two went back into the hall and to their waiting women. The food had already been served. Estella was picking at it, a disdainful expression slipping across her face now and then. Oyo was looking pleased with her work. She was

134

not eating much herself, but sat watching over everybody else. The men ate silently. Something had gone out of Koomson, and throughout the evening it did not come back. Now it was his wife Estella who talked, rambling on about the busy life of parties, and the names of important people fell from her lips with a frequency that had Oyo looking at her with envy and self-pity. Yet the man could see that Oyo was happy. Taking out those glasses and plates seemed to have brought her closer to the things she would like to spend her life doing, and to have given her the kind of self-respect she hungered for. Involuntarily, the man drifted off into old dreams of what he would like to do for her. In the end he was left feeling he would never be capable of doing what was necessary.

The old woman had been sitting throughout the desultory meal, staring at the silent Koomson as if she wanted to be ready to catch his first words should he decide to speak. But the Party man did not appear about to say anything. Finally, her smile bursting with her worship, the old woman spoke.

'Minister,' she began. Koomson turned to look at her. His eyes were the eyes of a man whose mind was entirely absent from that place and time. 'Minister,' the old woman said, 'it is nothing at all that I want to talk about. You know much better than I myself what has brought us together tonight.'

'Oh, yes,' said Koomson. He was making efforts at concentrating on the old woman's words. 'Oh, yes.'

'It is about the Ahead . . .' said the old woman.

'The what?' asked Koomson.

'She means the fishing boat,' said Oyo. 'That is the name for them here.'

'I see, I see,' said Koomson, nodding vigorously now.

'And so that is what I wanted to ask you about, Minister,' said the old woman.

'Ah, yes,' Koomson said, leaning forward in his seat.

'Things are very difficult these days. Very difficult.'

A long sigh rose from Estella. 'It's this foolish socialism that will spoil everybody's peace.'

'What is wrong with this socialism?' the man interrupted. Estella laughed.

'What is wrong, he asks. What is wrong, indeed!'

'Perhaps you know things we do not know,' said the man, very calmly.

'It is a nuisance,' said the Party man, following the statement with an uncertain laugh. 'It is not possible here.'

'But isn't it the thing you people say you believe in?'

Koomson laughed outright now. 'The old man himself does not believe in it. But when people see you doing something to get ahead, they become jealous and shout the slogans against you.'

'Just because they are jealous,' said Estella with indignation.

The old woman cleared her throat. The conversation seemed to have confused her completely. 'Is it about the boat you are talking?' she asked apologetically.

'Yes,' said Koomson. 'Now take this boat business, for instance. There is a lot of money to be made in it, but start something, and fools will start shouting slogans at you.' There was a certain genuine passion behind his words now, and the sweat forming over his brow made him look angry.

'So they won't allow you to buy the boats?' the old woman asked, pained.

'It is very difficult,' Koomson answered. 'It is difficult, but perhaps we can manage.'

'And . . .' the old woman paused, trying to decide whether it would be a mistake to ask, then 'how much is a boat?'

Koomson and his wife exchanged glances. Finally, he frowned and said, 'The smallest ones cost about twelve thousand pounds.'

'Ei, but that is real money!' shouted the old woman, grasping her belly.

'You have said it,' purred Estella, in a voice that was not hers.

'So many thousands!'

'Yes. But the money is not the difficult thing. After all, the Commercial Bank is ours, and we can do anything,' said Koomson.

'Mmmmm,' the old woman nodded.

'But they say we are socialist ministers, so we shouldn't do these things.'

The old woman almost leaped up with indignation. 'And so as for ministers, don't they also eat? Foolishness, just foolishness.'

'So you are not allowed to own these things?' Oyo asked.

'Don't mind them!' Estella's voice had climbed to its usual pitch. 'Do you know, they themselves, the ones who shout, own things, lots of things!'

Koomson gave his wife an under-brow glance, as if to say she was saying things that were not to be said, but then he himself added, 'Well, not in their own names, of course.'

'And now,' Estella added, 'they can't even use their wives' names. They say it spoils the Party's name.'

'Foolishness! Complete foolishness!' fumed the old woman.

'So what is to be done?' asked Oyo. There was a long silence, during the whole of which the man could not help smiling softly to himself. And then Koomson broke the silence. 'Of course if we can get somebody to . . .' he giggled childishly, 'er, lend us the name, then of course it would be a kind of partnership.' Another nervous laugh.

'Aaaah, we can talk about it,' said the old woman, uncertain now.

'If you would like to come in, we shall see,' said Koomson.

'Yes, we shall see,' the old woman repeated.

'It's just a matter of signing some papers, and knowing what to do, that is all,' said Koomson.

The man sat staring at the little group in the center of the room. He was tapping a noiseless rhythm on the table.

'But will there be any profit in it?' he asked. The question seemed to have taken everybody by surprise, but once asked, it hung there in the air and would not just go away. Koomson shifted in his seat.

'Well,' he frowned, 'it has been said that one of these boats can bring in a thousand pounds pure profit every year.'

'How, pure profit?' the man asked. The old woman was staring at him, and winking with furious speed, but he ignored her.

137

'I mean,' said Koomson, 'after maintenance and crew pay and that sort of thing.'

'Not the whole cost of the boat itself?'

'Oh no, how possible?'

'I see, I see.' The man put his right thumb up against his nose and pressed it down, flattening his nose in such a way that when he spoke, his voice came out through his constricted nostrils. 'In that case, before you earn enough to pay the price of the boat, it will be twelve years. I see.' He kept his thumb pressed down on his nose.

'I thought . . .' the old woman began. But in the middle of what she was about to say, something seemed to have struck her mind, and she stopped, her mouth open, her face looking extremely old.

'What matters,' came the high voice of Koomson's wife, 'is that there will be plenty of fish to eat. You know, fish is foully expensive these days.'

Koomson seemed unable to take his eyes off his watch now, and when he was able to catch his wife's eye he said, 'Estie, how about it?'

'We really have to go now,' said his wife, rising. The old woman seemed totally perplexed, then she too rose, and shook Estella's hand.

'B-but when shall we see you, for the papers and all?' she asked.

'Oh yes, Estie, when are we free?'

'You know you're always busy with your friends. Ah, perhaps Saturday.'

'Saturday,' repeated the old woman.

'But you have to come before six. Joe has to see some friends at the Atlantic-Caprice just after six.'

'Saturday, before six,' the old woman said, and she managed a sad smile. The Koomsons shook hands again.

'We'll prepare for you,' Estella said, smiling like a queen. The group went out into the night. The man walked slowly behind everybody else, saying nothing.

Outside, the driver was still hunched over the big car's wheel. To escape the cold night air he had rolled up the glass windows, and this made it hard for Koomson to wake him up. Estella banged angrily on the glass. The driver woke up, apologized, and stepped out to open the door for the Party man and his wife. The man, his wife and his mother-in-law waved good-bye, and with a soft sound of prosperity the car poured itself down the night, only an escaping shimmer of red lights in the blackness all around.

The old woman sighed a long sigh when the little family group returned into the hall.

'Aaaah, Koomson has done well, we must say it. He has done well for himself, and for his family too.' Neither the man nor his wife said anything to that.

'It is late,' said Oyo.

'Yes, indeed, it is,' said the old woman. 'I am going.'

'I will go with you, at least part of the way,' said Oyo.

At short intervals the old woman gave vent to a kind of subdued growl, as if there were things knocking against her breast, demanding exit. The man walked out to the veranda with them. 'I must say,' the old woman began at last, 'I must say that there are men somewhere in Ghana who at least know how to take good care of their own.' The man restrained himself, and the growls of displeasure continued from the old woman. 'People who can do manly things, and take the burdens of others too.'

Now the man laughed softly and said, 'Yes, we shall be rolling in fish.' The old woman spat violently against the earth. 'And you will have a boat in twelve years, perhaps.' The man's wife pulled his arm, and he said nothing more.

'Foolishness,' muttered the old woman. 'Sheer foolishness.' The man turned back. His good-night went ringing through the night, unanswered, and he thought he heard something said about useless men.

CHAPTER ELEVEN

He would have stopped the first taxi that came along, but his wife pointed out that it was foolish to pay so much money and not have the pleasure of sitting in a decent car. So he waited there by the roadside with her till one appeared of which the woman approved.

'This one,' she said. The man flagged down the passing vehicle. It was a new kind of car altogether, and when they were inside and it had started moving off, he asked the driver about it.

'They call it a Toyota,' said the driver. 'Japanese.'

'They have done well, the Japanese,' the man said.

'You have said it, brother,' answered the taxi driver. 'The way things are going, it seems everybody is making things now except us. We Africans only buy expensive things.'

The man did not continue the conversation. There really was nothing to say to that. Besides, he could sense that his wife was irritated by the taxi driver's natural familiarity, as if his speaking in this free, open manner with her husband took something away from her.

The driver sped along the road like an afternoon breeze, and he seemed to know where the man and his wife wanted to go. It was only when he came to the bridge over the lagoon that he asked where they were going.

'Go to the Upper Residential Area, driver,' said Oyo. 'On the hills beyond the new Esikafo Aba Estates.'

'Yes, Auntie.'

Oyo had leaned forward in order to deliver her instructions to the driver. The words 'Upper Residential Area' and 'Esikafo Aba Estates' had come dancing out of her mouth, and the man knew she had been turning them over long before the driver had thought of asking, savoring the sound, perfecting the way she was going to say her piece. And of course she had answered the driver's question with the perfect delivery of people who want it understood that in spirit, at least, they too belong to such areas. The taxi driver, too, had begun to speak to her as if he now understood her greatness. After all, it was not everybody who had some place to go in the Upper Residential Area. White men, then the old lawyers, and now the bigger Party men and a few civil servants. It was certainly not every fool who could get up and say he wanted to go to that area. Oyo had been quick to notice the new respect and admiration in the driver's tone. She fell back deep into the cushion behind her and relaxed contentedly.

Traveling, even a short ride in a taxi, had a very noticeable effect on Oyo. In the past this had disturbed the man, and he had thought of it as some form of disease, a childhood thing his wife had never really grown out of. She would sit there, in the train, in the bus, or, as now, in the taxi, and the way she behaved, anyone seeing her for the first time then would think it was her life, this hopping into taxis and being spoken to like a great woman. And then she would talk, bringing up the few rich things that had happened to her all her life, and some that had not really happened, some that had not even almost happened, and she would talk about these things as if they were absolutely the only things that ever happened in her life, a string of fabulous happenings. Somehow, it was most often in taxis and buses and trains that she brought up the subject of distant relatives who had money and power. The man had talked to Teacher, his friend, about this, but he had laughed and said Oyo was not alone, that the whole world was in the habit of pretending that their dreams were true in certain chosen places. Still, the man had not been able to get completely used to this thing in his wife. Now she was sitting back in the taxi seat as if she herself owned a dozen of these things. In a moment she was chuckling, the kind of bloodless chuckle that is intended to lead into something the chuckler is itching to say. The man closed his eyes, pretending sleep. Perhaps he could avoid the show. But the woman converted her small chuckle into a big laugh, and it was no longer possible for the man to play at being asleep. So he opened one eye, and his wife seized the opportunity.

'Grace is so funny.' Every syllable from her mouth was oiled with unfelt mirth.

'Yes,' said the man. It might be possible to cut off the display with the kind of agreement that kills any conversation. But Oyo was determined now.

'Aaah, cousin Grace!' she proceeded relentlessly. 'Did I show you the latest postcard she sent me from London?'

'Months ago you showed it to me, yes.'

There was a momentary flash of fury in the woman's eyes. The man caught the driver's eye in the rearview mirror, fascinated eyes.

'No!' said Oyo, 'I wasn't speaking about that one. That was when she was in Brussels. Don't you remember?'

'No.' The man closed his eyes. That way he would not see the accusing look his wife was sure to give him. The woman seemed to have accepted defeat for the moment. The happiness had disappeared completely from her voice.

A signboard, made out of slender vertical planks with the inscription ESIKAFO ABA ESTATES, slipped by. The taxi wound its way through a series of narrow, twisting roads between rows of identical houses, story apartments each with its detached servants' quarters, and through half-open eyes the man thought he could see his wife squint pensively and bite her lower lip as she watched the houses sliding past. He closed his eyes tight.

'We have arrived,' the driver said.

The man opened his eyes in time to see another signboard: UPPER RESIDENTIAL AREA. This one was small, and the lettering on it was neat and studied. The driver slowed down, hesitating at a parting in the road. The man told him to go straight on, and as the big houses with their high hedges drew nearer and disappeared behind the car, the driver asked for more instructions at every turn, and even began to ask a few questions of his own.

'And what does it mean at all, the name?' he asked.

'What name?' asked the man.

'The name of this place,' said the driver, laughing and adding,

'I have never been able to pronounce it properly. I didn't stay long in school, you know.'

'Oh, the Residential Area?'

'Yes.'

The man turned the name over in his mind, thinking of an explanation that would not sound too foolish. 'It means a place where people live.'

The driver made a half turn and gave the man a swift look halfway between laughter and unbelief. Then he chuckled. 'What do you mean, péople?' he asked.

'That is what it says. A place where people, human beings, have their houses.'

'But then every area is like that. So what is the use of the name?'

'Man, don't ask me,' laughed the man. The car was approaching Koomson's house, and he told the driver to stop in front of it. He paid the fare and helped his wife out, then as the car disappeared the two entered the gate cut through the high cement wall. The man stood by patiently as his wife stopped to look at the ironwork of the gate, tubes framed in the design of a rising sun, painted blue and gold. She stared at the gate with the longing interest of a woman thinking of getting herself something exactly like that as soon as she could. The man looked away, contemplating nothing in particular.

'Why do you make it impossible for me to speak to you?' the woman asked as they walked toward the house.

'What are you talking about?' the man asked.

'You know what I mean.'

'In the taxi?'

'Yes, in the taxi,' said his wife. 'Why do you always do that?'

'Oyo, you remember these things I don't remember, that's all.' The woman uttered a sound of complete exasperation, as if she were trying hard to contain her anger but knew it would be impossible. The two traversed the big garden in front of the house in total silence. Near the wall on the far side a gardener, very tall and thin, so that he seemed to bend like a reed, was watering an expanse of lush grass. His face was completely

143

covered with a mesh of thin lines cut into the flesh, and he was singing in a voice that was low and calm, except for an occasional sharp cry that rose and separated itself from the main song. Around a corner of the house a young girl in blue jeans and a light yellow shirt came riding, stopping just as she was about to run into the two.

'Who are you?' The girl spoke English like a white child, with the fearless, direct look of a white child.

'We are looking for your father,' answered the man.

'Daddy's upstairs,' said the girl. Immediately, absorbed in her own world, she turned her machine around and disappeared in the direction she had come from.

The door was opened by a servant girl, about sixteen years old. She had a sweet face, but her body was awkward and she held herself stiffly, smiling with a peculiar shyness, as if the thing she wanted to do most was to disappear.

'Please sit down,' she said, indicating a whole array of chairs and sofas. 'They are coming.' Then she went off through a back door.

The two, left alone, were at first too busy taking in the sight of the room they were in to say anything to each other. The man looked wonderingly at all the things in there. He was trying to avoid a direct meeting of eyes, but every now and then he became aware that his wife was doing the same thing, inspecting the room, and it seemed to him that more than once he happened to catch in her eyes the glint of a keen desire. He could not blame her in the least. There were things here for a human being to spend a lifetime desiring. There were things here to attract the beholding eye and make it accept the power of their owner. Things of intricate and obviously expensive design. It was impossible not to notice the ashtrays, for instance, since they were not just things to be used, but also things with a beauty of their own that forced the admiration of even the unwilling. How could a man be right in the midst of all this, wanting these things against which the mind sought to struggle? It was not the things themselves, but the way to arrive at them which brought so much confusion to the soul. And everybody knew the chances of finding a way that was not

144

rotten from the beginning were always ridiculously small. Many have found it worthwhile to try the rotten ways, and in truth there was no one living who had the strength to open his mouth to utter blame against them. Many had tried the rotten ways and found them filled with the sweetnesses of life. The rest were waiting for their turn, an opening along the same old ways. Even those who started out with a certain wholeness in their persons, it was funny with what predictability they got themselves ready eventually to give up and go. Men have thought they had no use for the sweetnesses, their own personal selves. But for all such men there have been ways to get to the rotten, sweet ways.

For the children.

Like a sidelong refrain that phrase jumped to the mind, a remembrance of past conversations with men who had eventually come to the end of their resistance. For the children. Supposing Deede also could have beautiful clothes with their beauty crossing the seas from thousands of miles away, and supposing Adoley could have a machine to ride around on, to occupy her attention while she was growing up, what would they know about ways that were rotten in the days of disappeared parents? What would they care? What, indeed, would anybody care?

For the little children.

In the end, was there anything done for the children's sake which could really be seen as a crime? Anything that could justify their condemnation to pain when all that was required was the sacrifice of something which would turn out in the end to be merely a fraction of life? After all, the people's acceptance of all these things was from a certain knowledge of what life itself is. Was there not some proverb that said the green fruit was healthy, but healthy only for its brief self? That the only new life there ever is comes from seeds feeding on their own rotten fruit? What then, was the fruit that refused to lose its acid and its greenness? What monstrous fruit was it that could find the end of its life in the struggle against sweetness and corruption?

It was amazing how much light there was in a place like this.

145

It glinted off every object in the room. Next to each ashtray there were two shiny things: a silver box and a small toy-like pistol. The man wondered what the pistols were for. Light came off the marble tops of the little side tables. People had wondered what use a State Marble Works Corporation could be. They need not have wondered. There were uses here.

The room itself was only half of a larger space. To the right of the door was what seemed to be the dining room, though whenever he turned round in his seat to look at it, all the man could see was a row of glass-covered shelves and with a multitude of polished dishes and glasses. The sitting room was cut off by a long, high frame, beautifully polished, also with shelves all covered with small, intricate objects that must have come from foreign lands, though of what use they were the man could not decide. To his own left there was one of the new television sets, and then farther on the corner was filled by two large contraptions whose outsides were of highly polished wood. One of them the man recognized as a radio set, though it was amazingly large. The other he found impossible to place. Then there were five deep, soft chairs, all with red cushions, and a carpet on the noiseless floor. There were also the two sofas, on one of which his wife was sitting.

When the man's gaze came to rest on his wife, he saw her looking as if she had been waiting a long time for a chance to say something to him.

'Mama would have come with us,' she said. But the man said nothing and she continued, 'Mama would have come if she hadn't been afraid you would laugh at her.'

'I wonder which of us is in a position to laugh longest at the other.'

'I get angry when you make fun of her,' she said.

'Oyo,' he said, 'if you long to quarrel, try someone else.'

'The boat is a very serious thing to her,' she said. 'You don't seem to see that.'

'Oh, I see it all right.'

'So why do you make fun of her?'

'I think she is being fooled, that's all,' he said. 'And you with her.'

146

'You don't need to act so happy about it, do you?' she asked.

'You two are happy. Why should I be the one to cry?' The woman looked as if she would say something really indignant, but at that moment there was a voice from the stairs behind.

'We've been having a long nap,' said Koomson, descending. 'Such a busy night, last night. We had to go to three different nightclubs.' He was in his dressing gown, a shiny thing in its own right, and he had not finished wrapping himself up in it.

'Good evening, Minister,' smiled Oyo.

'Good evening,' answered Koomson, beaming with self-esteem. Almost in the same breath, he called out: 'Atinga!' It was a peculiar kind of shout, the kind made by white men trying to pronounce African names without any particular desire to pronounce them well, indeed deriving that certain superior pleasure from their inability. The shout was answered by a loud 'Sah!' from somewhere in the back, and in a moment a thin, short man, about fifty, stood at the back door, awaiting his master's instructions. He wore a white drill shirt and trousers with red bands running down the sides. Without appearing to take the least notice of the steward, Koomson walked over to the big radio in the corner and turned the receiver on. A voice like thunder shook the air, and Koomson slowly turned down the volume.

'There is nothing to beat a German set,' he said.

'There's someone waiting over there,' the man said, indicating the steward.

'Oh, the steward boy,' Koomson said, still playing with the loud noises from his huge toy. 'By the way, what will you drink?'

'Anything will do.'

'Oh, you must choose,' said Koomson. 'There's White Horse, you know. Black and White, Seagram's, Gilbey's Dry . . .'

'Anything will do,' the man repeated, his voice deliberately dull.

'Well, I'll let you choose, then,' said Koomson. 'Atinga,

bring the trolley, and put different drinks. Put also ice, put glasses, four.'

'Yessah!' said Atinga, withdrawing through the door.

'Estie will be down in a moment,' Koomson said. He gave the knob on the receiver another turn, and the deep, softly insistent bass of a high life tune replaced the first meaningless sounds. The steward came in with all the different bottles and the ice and the glasses on the trolley, pushing it before him with reverent motions, and served the man and his wife some of the whisky. Mrs Koomson descended the stairs, wearing a dress that seemed to catch each individual ray of light and aim it straight into the beholding eye. She, like her husband, did not take a drink. She sat languidly in her chair, and for some time she did nothing but stroke her wig from front to back in motions that were long, slow, and very studied.

'Is that the dining room?' Oyo asked, pointing.

'Yes,' said Estella. 'They have come for the furniture.'

'They?'

'The State Furniture Corporation. They renew it for us. Joe is like this with the manager.'

'I see.' There were questions in Oyo's eyes, questions that probably would have sprung from envy and admiration, but she did not ask them. Instead, she turned the conversation. 'I didn't know your first born had become such a young lady. What is her name?'

'Princess,' said Estella.

'Is that her real name, or some sort of nickname?' asked the man.

'It's her name,' said Estella, giving the man a supercilious look.

'I was a tight friend of your sister Regina, when we were in school,' Oyo said.

'She's in London now.'

'What is she doing?'

'She has a scholarship. Joe arranged it for her.'

'Is she in a university, then?' asked the man.

'No,' Estella said. 'She's specializing in dressmaking. She

148

says she's going to name her establishment after me when she comes. Estic Models, London Trained.'

'She is very lucky,' said Oyo.

'She is a very funny girl,' said Estella, with a small, hard laugh. 'She says she has fallen in love with a Jaguar, and she's going to kill herself if she can't have it. She wants us to get her the foreign exchange for it.'

'I thought that was no longer possible,' said the man, looking at Koomson.

'Everything is possible,' Koomson said. 'It depends on the person.'

'Hmm.' The man could have opened his mouth again, to talk of the irony of it all, of people being given power because they were good at shouting against the enslaving things of Europe, and of the same people using the same power for chasing after the same enslaving things. He could have asked if anything was supposed to have changed after all, from the days of chiefs selling their people for the trinkets of Europe. But he thought again of the power of the new trinkets and of their usefulness, and of the irresistible desire they brought. He thought of his own children's longing for things, and of the satisfaction of Koomson's little Princess, and he said nothing.

Koomson walked over to the large thing beside the radio set. He lifted the top of it and pressed something inside it. Then he reached over and stopped the music from the radio.

'What is that?' asked Oyo. At times she had the ability to make herself sound exactly like an admiring villager. A trick to please.

'Oh, that's the recorder,' Estella replied before her husband could say anything. 'Sometimes the music from the radio is no music at all. With the tape recorder we only listen to what we want.'

Organ music, deep and voluminous, filled the room, and Estella, as if this Sunday music had really moved her soul, closed her eyes, breathing in deeply. Koomson looked up, frowning.

'It's getting late,' he said. 'I'll get the papers.' He was back in a few minutes, with a little file in his hand.

'I thought it was the old lady who was going to sign,' he said.

'Mama couldn't come,' said Oyo. 'She isn't feeling very well.' She looked at the man with a look that seemed both to defy him and to beg him not to contradict her. 'We can sign for her.'

'I don't think I can sign,' said the man. Oyo stared at him in amazement and disappointment. But the moment was brief, and therefore almost entirely private.

'I will sign it,' said Oyo.

Afterward the two of them, the man and his wife, waited in silence for Koomson and his wife to get ready and come down again. After a long wait they came. The four went out into the big car, and the chauffeur drove off.

'You know where Kwesi Anan lives?' Koomson asked the chauffeur.

'Yessah.'

'Good. Take us there first.' Then turning to Oyo in the back seat, he explained, 'Kwesi Anan is the head crewman on the boat.'

The crewman lived very close to the fishing harbor, in a room at the extreme end of a long, low house. It was already quite dark in his room, so that when he was called he came out squinting against the weak dusk light, muttering something loud and involved, something which seemed to mean that he was sorry he had no place to take the visitors to, that his room was not a room at all, only a converted lavatory.

'Greet the lady here,' said Koomson. 'She will be looking after the boat when I am not here. Do not forget her face.'

The young man peered into Oyo's face, then into the man's, and nodded his satisfaction.

'Driver, you know where we went last Sunday?' Koomson asked.

'Yessah!'

'Go there.'

The car sped smoothly along the coast road. Its own smooth running mixed with the soft sounds of the sea flowing over the sands. The man closed his eyes, and like a piece of twine the

150

thought ran round and round inside his head that it would never be possible to look at such comfortable things and feel a real contempt for them. Envy, certainly, but not contempt. So how was a man ever going to be able to fight against all the things and all the loved ones who never ceased urging that nothing else mattered, that the way was not important, that the end of life was the getting of these comfortable things? For the self, or if not for the self, then for the loved ones, or the children. Nothing else mattered.

CHAPTER TWELVE

The boat did not in fact leave as long a shadow as the man had feared it might. Occasionally, when on a breezy day he happened to wander in the direction of the fishing harbor, he saw it lying there upon the blue-green water of the sea, with the name of Koomson's little daughter lettered neatly in the front of it: PRINCESS. Every time he saw it, he could not help thinking how very beautiful the boat was. Then he would come home with the desire to talk to Oyo about the beauty of the day and all the boats in the harbor growing strong in him, but he knew it would bring her more pain and disappointment than happiness, so in the end he never said anything about his feelings and his thoughts.

Even the old woman seemed gradually to have resigned herself to the knowledge that what Koomson had come offering her was not the rainbow that would forever end the darknesses of her life and her daughter's life. This realization did not, indeed, end her bitterness toward the man. It deepened it, as if in some ultimate way the old woman had no doubt at all that the man had willed her disappointment. The man, for his part, was content to note again how unwilling the powerless became when there was a call for them to resent the powerful. Once it seemed that Oyo's old hopes were about to rise again, in a pathetic, unpleasant way. But they too died, leaving only their ashes. What happened was that from time to time Koomson would remember the ones who were supposed to be, for the eyes and ears of the prying world, the owners of his boat, and send one of his drivers with some fish for Oyo's mother or for Oyo herself. Even with the knowledge that was now in them, the women were grateful for these gifts, with a childish gratitude mixed with unreal hopes and desires.

The man had come home from work tired but not unhappy. Oyo had given him a supper of fish and *kenky*, and with a good appetite he had begun to eat. But quite suddenly, as if she had been moved by something she could not resist, Oyo said to him, 'That fish came straight from Koomson's boat.'

The man could not think of anything to say. There was something in the air around the words that filled them with a certain unhealthiness. The man just chewed the piece in his mouth over and over again, till the taste was all lost.

'After all, it was not for nothing, the signing.'

Beneath his tongue the man felt something like a sharp sting. He turned away from the table and said softly to his wife, 'Please don't cook any more fish for me.'

It was impossible to see the look in Oyo's eyes. She had turned them down, so that the light shone off the top of her forehead and the broad upper part of her nose. The corners of her mouth seemed to move very gently in a movement that may have had more to do with pity for herself than with hatred for the man. The terrible feeling of loneliness again came over him in his own home, and he walked out with a desperation that was no less deep for all its suddenness, groping through the night for the only human hand that could touch his and not make him feel a stranger to life.

But after that it never happened again, and to the extent that it was possible to forget these things, what had taken place was forgotten. Perhaps the Koomsons themselves tired of the necessity of sending the parcels of fish. Perhaps Oyo had them all sent to her mother, who ate her own bitterness and did not come so often now to her son-in-law, searching for the root of it. There was now, if nothing else, a willingness among the loved ones to accept the failure of the beloved. It may not have produced flights of happiness and self-esteem, but there was something at least comforting in the knowledge that people were not choking with expectations of great things from the impotent. Otherwise, life was just like that, just life. A little rumble now and then, even one big one every long while. But at this late time the watching eye and the listening ear knew better than to think there could be any upheaval which would not end up leaving things the way they had always been. Now the man knew he was beginning to understand the nature of everybody's progress into the grave. When all hopes had grown into disappointments, there would be no great unwillingness about the final going.

There was a lot of noise, for some time, about some investigation designed to rid the country's trade of corruption. De-uncorrupt themselves? There was nobody around who was all that excited; though of course men were willing to talk of the commission. The head of it was a professor from Legon. From Legon, they said, in order to give weight and seriousness to the enterprise. In the end it was being said in the streets that what had to happen with all these things had happened. The net had been made in the special Ghanaian way that allowed the really big corrupt people to pass through it. A net to catch only the small, dispensable fellows, trying in their anguished blindness to leap and to attain the gleam and the comfort the only way these things could be done. And the big ones floated free, like all the slogans. End bribery and corruption. Build Socialism. Equality. Shit. A man would just have to make up his mind that there was never going to be anything but despair, and there would be no way of escaping it, except one. That could wait. Meanwhile the days could go on and on like this. A man could learn to live with many, many things before the end. Many, many things.

CHAPTER THIRTEEN

In the early morning the man let the world around him lose itself in the growing pattern of the railway graph above the desk in front of him. Sometimes he could forget himself and almost everything else, concerning himself with the job alone, doing everything that was necessary. It was not difficult so to forget the self and the world against which it had to live. At least the job itself was one of the few around which did not have a killing dullness. There really was a definite kind of beauty to the growth of the daily maze on the graph sheet, and a satisfaction in seeing the penciled lines crossing the time and station lines, red lines for passenger trains, lead pencil lines for goods trains, blue for manganese. There was not that kind of dullness in the job, and that was something good.

Sometimes he took little trips to the Accident Room, to give the senior men there some files needed in the investigation of derailments and things of that sort. Once he had actually had to work there, relieving a man who had gone on leave in the countryside and then extended his free time by sending a long series of telegrams claiming the death of one after the other of a whole clan of relatives. The job was a filing job, and he had discovered that there were only about thirty letters a day needing to be put away, most probably never to be looked at again in one human life when one file was completed. There was enough real work there for about three-quarters of an hour, and then all a person had left to do was to sit in the office feeling the sweat on his back running down the small into the space around his anus. When the filing clerk returned from his long leave of funerals he was looking uncommonly cheerful, and all he would do when people gave him their sympathy for his dead ones was to crack for their benefit a small, understanding smile, as if it was he who was in a position to pity them. Later, the man had tried to find out how this clerk managed to fill a whole civil service day with the little work he was given to do. What he had found out was that the clerk had a meticulous system for stretching out his work, and he had done it so often and gotten so used to it that he had probably forgotten that most of it was merely a way to waste time. Alphabetical listings that would never serve any purpose; a search to try and find on the postmark the exact minute every letter was supposed to have been mailed; three transfers of all the lists to cleaner paper, each time in more careful, more beautiful lettering, with not a single smudge: periodic visits to the lavatory, from habit, not necessity.

Most jobs were like that, the man knew. People spent whole days behind desks, and like any civil servant, if some woman come from a village wanting to know such things and asked them straight what exactly it was they spent their time doing, they would never be able to give a real answer. A job was a job. It did not matter at all that nothing was done on most jobs.

He was alone now. Whenever he found himself alone and became aware of his loneliness, it was in the form of a peculiar sound. The sound was a high-pitched note, almost too high to be heard, and in fact audible only because what was in the ear could not be the sound of complete silence. He listened to this sound, wondering whether he could make it change and sound louder by concentrating on it. Then the telephone rang and he answered it, breaking the lonely sound.

It was not until after eight o'clock that the other staff started coming in. When, at half past seven, not even the messengers had come, the man had wondered what could have happened, but in a while he took his mind off the matter. The messengers were, as usual, the first to arrive. One of them came in like a ghost, so quietly in fact that the man did not notice him till the other arrived. This one came whistling, which was something of an unusual thing to do, though it did not disturb the man. But the other messenger shut his companion up. The second could not bear the silence long, and, walking around behind the man, he sighed very loudly and exclaimed, 'Ei, these *coups!*'

The man did not turn around, but he asked the messenger, 'Has there been another one?'

'Yea, man!'

'In Africa or somewhere else?'

'Today, today, here in Ghana!'

Now the other messenger walked out of his corner and joined the two. 'So you haven't heard?'

'On the morning shift we can't hear the news,' the man said.

'No six o'clock news this morning. Only some strange announcement by a man with a strange name, then *soja* music. They say they have seized power.'

'Who?' the man asked.

'Army men and policemen.'

'Oh, I see. I thought they always had power. Together with Nkrumah and his fat men.'

The messengers said nothing. Even the one who had come in whistling had a sort of second fear in his eyes, the kind of look people have when they are unsure of what they are doing, and want to take care to be able to claim that it was all a joke, should the need arise. In the man's own mind there was a diffuse uncertainty. What, after all, could it mean? One man, with the help of people who loved him and believed in him, had arrived at power and used it for himself. Now other men, with the help of guns, had come to this same power. What would it mean?

The senior men did not come to work. Fear was a very strong thing in their lives, and it was understandable that they would want to wait when something like this was happening. In the great strike many men had thought the big chance had definitely come, and had rushed to say how much they had fought against the order they thought had been overthrown. When in the end the police came and dragged people off to their jails and everyone knew there would be no change, many senior men had walked around fearing that someone who had heard them in the red days would remember their words.

The other junior staff came one by one, adding little bits, some very wild indeed, to the news available. They said all big Party men were being arrested and placed in something called protective custody – already a new name for old imprisonment without trial. New people, new style, old dance. When the Time Allocations clerk came in, he greeted everybody loudly and added, in a highly satisfied tone, 'Now another group of bellies will be bursting with the country's riches!' The reaction to that, like everything else this day, was a confusion of approval and insecure hesitation.

When the sun had gone up there was the sound of some commotion in the street outside. A man who had been a trade unionist for the overthrown government rushed into the office announcing the *coup* as if he had himself accomplished it. Then he ordered people to go out and show their loyalty to the new men of power. With a silence that spoke everybody's shame, the men in the office went out singly to join the crowd outside. In the same manner they had gone out in fear to hear the farts of the Party men.

The man did not move from his desk. The old-new union man stood staring at him, then said, 'Contrey, what about you?'

'Yes, what about what?'

'We are all demonstrating.'

'For what?'

'Don't you know there is a new government?'

'They tell me so. But I know nothing about the men. What will I be demonstrating for?'

'Look, contrey, if you don't want trouble, get out.'

'If two trains collide while I'm demonstrating, will you take the responsibility?'

'Oh,' said the organizer, 'if it is the job, fine. But we won't tolerate any Nkrumaists now.'

'You know,' said the man slowly, 'you know who the real Nkrumaists are.'

The unionist turned round and went down to join his crowd. Through the windows their sounds came: old songs with the words changed from the old praise for Nkrumah to insults for him. So like the noises of the Party when all the first promise had been eaten up and it had become a place where fat men found things to swell themselves up some more. The noise moved away up the hill, and then the men who had followed their fear to go and swell it did not come back to work the rest

158

of the day. The time had a quietness that raised thoughts of the man's whole life, with images and even tastes that struck the senses with a painful sharpness and then disappeared immediately, leaving only the sense of something forever gone, an aloneness which not even death might end.

The evening shift man came only a few minutes late. He looked very preoccupied with some interior business, and he offered nothing, no information about the *coup*, except a long look of great chagrin and uncertainty. Perhaps, like all the ambitious, he had been hoping to realize some great personal dream of sudden wealth, and with the fall of the old government his dreams had had to disappear. Perhaps.

The streets were very quiet. Only here and there, a small group of men would be talking, and it did not seem necessarily true that they were talking of the things that had taken place this day. At the bus stop people were talking, but in truth nobody knew anything except that there had been a change, and the words merely repeated the talkers' first astonishment, then endless questions about who the new men were, what they were going to do, what they had been doing all along. There were no answers to any of these questions, though one man who reeked of drink and vomit claimed that this was all a plan of the devilish Nkrumah, to bring everybody out into the streets and then have his soldiers and his policemen catch them all and lock them up, as he had done before. Near Effia Nkwanta the bus backfired, and a woman passenger with a child in her arms threw herself forward, rushing toward the entrance and screaming that they were going to kill her and her little one. Otherwise there was nothing really unusual, except perhaps that there was more silence around, as if, in a rare moment, people were all busy thinking and had no time or no desire to fill the air with the usual noises of life. As he turned along the road to go home, the man felt completely apart from all that was taking place. He would like to know about it, but there would be plenty of time for it, and he was not burdened with any hopes that new things, really new things, were as yet ready to come out. Someday in the long future a new life would maybe flower in the country, but when it came, it would not

159

choose as its instruments the same people who had made a habit of killing new flowers. The future goodness may come eventually, but before then where were the things in the present which would prepare the way for it?

When he got home the man felt almost happy, and like a happy man he did not climb up the four little steps onto the veranda, but leaped lightly up, thinking of youth and days in school when the sun had shone sweetly in the fields.

He found that the single leap had almost ended in a collision with Oyo. She was standing just outside the hall door, and when he could see her face properly the man judged that she was confused. She was looking as if something tremendous were disturbing her, but at the same time the man could see in her eyes something he could only think of as a deep kind of love, a great respect. He continued his forward movement until he had pushed his wife back very gently against the wall to the side of the door. Though the movement and the sudden tenderness in himself surprised him, he knew it was true, and he put all his fingers deep into her hair and held her head, pressing against her and letting her feel his desire for her. She raised her eyes in a motion of soft unbelief, and she looked like a young girl afraid she may be doing something wrong.

Deede came out, making straight for the kitchen. It was impossible to see her face clearly, but she moved like a child greatly agitated. The man looked again into his wife's face.

'Let's go in,' he said.

'He is inside,' she said, with a wild look. 'Koomson.'

'When did he come?'

'About an hour, two hours.'

'But why?'

'They are arresting them. He fears they will kill him. It is terrible.'

She held his hand and led him inside, as if he were a stranger coming into her house, or a lover not sure of himself. Adoley and Ayivi were sleeping in the hall, entangled like some strange kind of Siamese twins in the same chair.

'They have eaten,' Oyo said. Then, again unnecessarily, she

160

motioned to him to come quietly, and the two of them entered the inner room.

It was quite dark inside. The smell was something the man had not at all expected. It was overpowering, as if come corrosive gas, already half liquid, had filled the whole room, irritating not only the nostrils, but also the inside, of eyes, ears, mouth, throat. It was difficult at first to tell where Koomson was in the darkness, so the man reached for the wall switch and turned on the light.

Koomson was sitting on the bed, just behind the screen. He looked like a man afraid that the utterance of a single word would be the end of him. He was in a suit of dark woolen material with a shirt whose brilliant whiteness had in the sudden light a tinge of blue, and a black bow tie. On his nose small points of perspiration stood, looking as if they were about to increase in size and fall every next moment. But they did not fall. Koomson sat rigid for a few moments, like a person knowing it was a matter of the greatest importance for him to avoid making any motion at all. Slowly, as if he were trying to do it without attracting the attention of invisible watchers, he raised his staring eyes in the direction of the light above, then looked imploringly at the man. Surprised, in spite of himself, by the completeness of the change in Koomson's manner, the man failed to understand the look. In a moment Koomson was gesturing with quick, desperate motions, pointing first at the light and then at the open window in his silent frenzy, the fear coming out of every piece of him.

The man understood. He switched off the light. Then he moved over to the window, pulled the shutters and closed them, straining for a breath of good air as he did so. He waited for Koomson to say something now, but only the subdued breathing of the frightened man, punctuated with increasing rapidity from below, destroyed the peace of the room. When the man's eyes had again adjusted to the darkness, he could see the vague luminosity of Koomson's eyes in the black space of his face. The eyes were still turned in the direction of the window, though from time to time they seemed to turn with a mad quickness toward the door, when any noise or any movement came from there. With time the whiteness of Koomson's shirt became discernible again, even seeming to supply a soft light of its own. Once the man thought he saw Koomson staring at his shirt front, as if he saw in that too another source of possible danger to himself. Seeing the Partyman there in front of him now, acting as if he saw himself entirely surrounded by hostile things and feared that every coming moment would turn out to be his last, the man remembered the last visit and wondered at the great contrast with the superconfidence of the days gone by. It would be wrong, very wrong, to think as he was already thinking, that the change would bring nothing new. In the life of the nation itself, maybe nothing really new would happen. New men would take into their hands the power to steal the nation's riches and to use it for their own satisfaction. That, of course, was to be expected. New people would use the country's power to get rid of men and women who talked a language that did not flatter them. There would be nothing different in that. That would only be a continuation of the Ghanaian way of life. But here was the real change. The individual man of power now shivering, his head filled with the fear of the vengeance of those he had wronged. For him everything was going to change. And for those like him who had grown greasy and fat singing the praises of their chief, for those who had been getting themselves ready for the enjoyment of hoped-for favors, there would be long days of pain ahead. The flatterers with their new white Mercedes cars would have to find ways of burying old words. For those who had come directly against the old power, there would be much happiness. But for the nation itself there would only be a change of embezzlers and a change of the hunters and the hunted. A pitiful shrinking of the world from those days Teacher still looked back to, when the single mind was filled with the hopes of a whole people. A pitiful shrinking, to days when all the powerful could think of was to use power of a whole people to fill their own paunches. Endless days, same days, stretching into the future with no end anywhere in sight.

There was a rasping noise from where Koomson sat. It seemed he had said something, but the man had not understood him.

'Did you say anything?' the man asked. Instantly, he saw Koomson recoil as if he feared that the sound of a normal voice could only be meant to betray him. The shiny eyes closed for a brief moment, then when they opened again Koomson seemed to have recovered from his fright and he leaned forward and whispered into the man's face, 'They will kill me.'

His mouth had the rich stench of rotten menstrual blood. The man held his breath until the new smell had gone down in the mixture with the liquid atmosphere of the Party man's farts filling the room. At the same time Koomson's insides gave a growl longer than usual, an inner fart of personal, corrupt thunder which in its fullness sounded as if it had rolled down all the way from the eating throat thundering through the belly and the guts, to end in further silent pollution of the air already thick with flatulent fear. Oyo had remained silent all this time, standing close to the door. But now, with a choking sound, she retreated into the hall outside.

The man himself was filled with only one thought now: to get out of this room. But there was Koomson sitting up on the bed, his body drawn up as if his greatest remaining wish was to grow smaller, to disappear if that would be possible.

'They will come here,' Koomson whispered again. This time the man was quick to pull his head back before the impact of the Party man's breath. Still, the smell waves came, a little delayed and only slightly less potent. The man wished Koomson could be struck suddenly dumb, but now silence was impossible.

'Did anyone see you come?' he asked.

'I don't know,' Koomson answered. Then, after a while, 'I think so.'

The man thought he would surely vomit if he did not get out from this foul smell. Hoping to steal a breath of uncorrupted air, he moved toward the window. But as he got ready to open the shutters, trying not to alarm Koomson, he heard a low, throaty murmur of distress. He left the window and went back to sit by the fugitive Minister, keeping a fruitless distance between himself and the other. He thought with some surprise of his complete inability to get affected by the feelings and fears of the figure next to him. There was only the awareness of his own acute discomfort, plus a certain resentment, small at first but growing much more noticeable with the moments, that in all his prosperous moments it was only now that the Party man should really want to get close to him. And the stink was insupportable.

'Do you think you want to take a bath?' the man asked.

'Oh no,' said Koomson promptly, his eyes moving as he shook his head. 'No, no,'

'Fine, fine,' said the man, feeling he was about to die of this smell. 'Do you want to go to the latrine first, then?'

There was a long pause. Then he heard Koomson sigh in the manner of a persecuted man, before saying, 'I don't feel like it.'

'Fine, fine,' the man said. The smell was truly unbearable.

As if to plead with him not to torment a poor fugitive with cruel questions, Koomson sighed again, a very long, slow sigh that spoke clearly of his suffering. Even a sigh from him spoiled the air some more. The man tried again, looking for a way out, any way out.

'Have you eaten?' he asked.

'No.'

The sound from Koomson was surprisingly hopeful. The man jumped up.

'I'll get Oyo to give you something,' he said. Without waiting for even the possibility of an answer, he threw himself out into the hall and took in the welcome air there in great grateful gasps.

Deede was still not asleep. She was sitting on the floor, in a corner beside the table, looking very tired. Oyo was seated at the big table, looking down at the top of it. She got up when she saw the man, and when he had come quite close she whispered in his ear, 'How he smells!'

'It is fear,' he said, trying to sound casual. 'He says he's hungry. What is there to eat?'

'Oh, and you yourself, you haven't eaten.'

'I don't feel hungry any more,' the man said. 'But we have to give him something to eat.'

Oyo led the way into the kitchen. There was still a low fire in the coal pot. When she had blown away the covering ash, she added some more charcoal to it. Then she fanned it until it was glowing again and heated the man's food. The man took it in and gave it to the hungry Party man.

Koomson ate in the darkness. It was again hard to see, since Koomson did not want the door open. Only the sounds coming from him told the man how eagerly he was eating. They were greedy noises, the sucking noises of an impatient man hungrily pushing food into his face. His fear must have increased his appetite. Now the man could leave him alone.

He went back into the hall and stood quietly beside Oyo. She held his hand in a tight grasp. Then, in a voice that sounded as if she were stifling, she whispered, 'I am glad you never became like him.'

In Oyo's eyes there was now real gratitude. Perhaps for the first time in their married life the man could believe that she was glad to have him the way he was. He returned the increasing pressure of her hand, then left her to take a glass of water to the man inside.

Koomson felt with a hand for the water. It made a hollow sound as it went down into his belly, and a wet belch rose from his throat.

At that moment the cloth at the window was illuminated, very briefly, be the light of a passing vehicle. The man heard a low moan from Koomson, then the sound of the engine that had passed died completely, to be replaced by the impact of boots on the hard road surface outside. The boots marching to a disciplined rhythm.

'They are coming,' said Koomson.

In the darkness his words themselves had sounded quite calm, but as soon as he had said them he was by the man, holding onto him like a frightened child. Without saying anything, the man took the shivering arm and pulled it gently after him.

In the hall Deede was now also asleep, and Oyo herself looked as if only fear was keeping her awake. It was clear that she had understood the noises outside, and the understanding had deepened her uncertainty almost to the point of panic. The man motioned to her not to move.

'Say I went out, alone, some time ago,' he said. 'You don't know where. Say nothing about him.' Oyo nodded hesitantly.

Koomson walked like a man without a will of his own. The man had almost to pull him, past the other doors and the wet area around the bathroom, into the latrine. Again the powerful smell, making the man think of particles of shit doing a wild, mixed dance with drops of stale urine in the small space of the latrine.

The man shut the door and pulled the bolt behind it, then switched on the little light. Koomson was looking up at the ceiling with something like relief. But there, nothing could be seen except cement that had once been painted over with a sick yellow, blackened in large places by the midnight candles of constipated men when the small bulb was burned out. The man saw Koomson lower his stare and look left at the window above the latrine seat. The window led outside, out of the yard, and was possibly large enough for a man to go through, even a man of Koomson's size. But the hole of the window had three upright iron bars stuck in it. Now these bars looked most unnecessary and cruelly strong. Koomson, sweating all over the fabric of his clothes, looked pathetically into the man's face.

The man looked silently down at the wooden box seat of the latrine. The shithole in the box was, as usual, encrusted with old caked excrement. Occasionally it would happen that some disgusted tenant would get up one day and give the seat a good cleaning. But this kind of thing was quite rare. Most of the time, the individual who went in there would be content to protect his single arse with a piece of newspaper he would use to wipe himself afterward.

'We can go out,' said the man, adding considerately, 'if you want to.'

'Here?' asked Koomson, pointing to the shithole. His voice was filled with his despair.

'Yes, here.'

The man held onto one end of the box seat and indicated the

other end with a motion of his hand. Koomson followed him, and held the free end. Together the two of them pulled at the box, trying to move it forward off the wall.

The thing did not move.

The man stooped to take a closer look at it where it came against the back wall. There were nails in it, fixing the box seat to the building. The man looked at Koomson.

'We can still try,' he said. But Koomson was very quiet.

The man pushed his left hand through the shithole.

'Help me push the can aside,' he said.

It took Koomson some time to make up his mind, but in the end, like a man at his own funeral, he stuck his hand in the other side of the hole and touched the can. Together they shifted it to one side. The touch of the can had something altogether unexpected about it. It was cold, but not at all wet or slippery. It felt instead as if a multitude of little individual drops had been drying on the can for ages, but had never quite arrived at a totally dry crispness. When the can itself was shifted, a new smell evaporated upward into the faces above the hole. It was rather mild, the smell of something like dead mud. A very large cockroach, its color a shiny, deep brown, flew out from under the can, hit Koomson's white shirt front and fell heavily on top of the box seat before crawling away into a crack down the side.

'We'll have to go through the latrine man's hole,' the man said. Koomson did not answer.

'You go first,' the man said. He felt he had to add something by way of explanation, so he added, 'If they come . . .'

Koomson just stood there.

'Go, man!'

The shout seemed to have awakened Koomson from some faraway place. He looked at the hole waiting for him with the powerless loathing of a defeated man, then he put his hands against the box, getting ready to push his feet down the hole. The man shook his head.

'You can't go that way,' he said softly. 'You'll get stuck.'

Koomson was hesitating. He did not seem to think there was anything else he could do now.

'Head first,' the man said. 'That is the only way.'

Disgust came strongly into Koomson's face, struggling to suppress his earlier resignation. Outside in the yard, the noises increased. Doors being knocked on and opened, brusque voices demanding to know something or other, softer voices answering with the deference of fear, hard steps on the cement of the yard. Once there was the brutal sound of a door giving in to the force of something heavy and hard.

The disgust left Koomson's face, and the resignation returned. With a small shudder he lowered his head till it was just above the hole, then in a rapid sinking action he thrust it through. He was beginning to cough as he tried to force his shoulders down. Then the movement stopped. The noises outside were getting louder, and they were much closer now. The voices of the searchers were clear now, and they sounded angry.

The man saw the Party man frantically kick his legs. Quickly he grasped the legs and pulled with all his force. Koomson's head hit the edge of the hole as he came out.

Without a word, the man rapidly got hold of Koomson's jacket and removed it. Koomson himself took off his tie. Then he went down the hole again, the disgust returning to share his face with his resignation.

This time Koomson's body slipped through easily enough, past the shoulders and down the middle. But at the waist it was blocked by some other obstacle. The man looked at the hole again, but there was space there. Perhaps the latrine man's hole outside was locked. The wooden latch securing it would be quite small, and should break with a little force.

'Push!' the man shouted, before he had thought of the nearness of the searchers, or of the fact that his companion could not hear him anyhow. Quietly now, he climbed onto the seat, held Koomson's legs and rammed them down. He could hear Koomson strain like a man excreting, then there was a long sound as if he were vomiting down there. But the man pushed some more, and in a moment a rush of foul air coming up told him the Party man's head was out. The body dragged itself painfully down, and the man got ready to follow into the hole.

His hands encountered small, rolled-up balls of earth that felt like the bits of soil thrown up by worms. The smell of cockroaches fought the human stench, and their droppings stuck to the man's elbows as he crawled through the interior of the box seat. Something that had an icky wetness made his right hand slip and entered the space underneath a fingernail, and he remembered the vomiting sound Koomson had made on his way down. The small door was open. With a last effort the man threw his head through it, then he relaxed as his body came after. The air outside was sweet again, even so near the hole. The sky above had no moon and no stars, though there was a diffused light that made the man suspect that the moon was only hidden.

Koomson was lying there beside him in the lane at the back of the latrine. The man held him and half lifted him. He walked with him through the lanes of the area, keeping away from the streets where they might have run into people.

CHAPTER FOURTEEN

The two men walked in the direction of the fishing harbor to the east. They kept to the little lanes between the walls around people's houses, going past the many latrine holes and their little gutters running with the dark liquid that could be smelled even in the darkness of the night, old mixtures of piss and shit. They were walking along the latrine man's circuit through life. A very small boy, unaccountably out of doors so late, squeezed past them in a lane. He hurried away from them, then, stopping at a safe distance, gave a long, disgusted shout. 'Foooooooh!' Then he ran from the two adults and disappeared around the last corner.

Where the houses ended the two men came to the open field. Ordinarily, to the walker looking across from the road, the field looked clear. But to the two walking across it now, avoiding any stray people they might have encountered on the road, the field seemed to offer nothing but stumps and holes and mounds. Koomson was walking like some wooden thing, not seeming to care where it was he was going, like a being for whom the world had ceased to exist.

Near the middle of the field there was a wide, flat, uncemented gutter which the man thought of avoiding by walking over toward the bus stop, near which the gutter bent westward under a small wooden bridge, to continue parallel to the road. But he could see vaguely the shapes of a small group of people waiting like neglected ghosts at the bus stop, perhaps for one of the small night trucks. So he took Koomson's arm and together they went across the gutter, their feet sinking now and then in places along the soft parts of the bottom, and on the other side they stamped upon the earth to get rid of some of the aged mud.

The old cans in their path were full of compacted mud, and they were so rotten with rust they made only a dull, flat sound when kicked. Occasionally what they kicked was not rusty metal, but bits of cracked coolers now also filled with moist mud, and little pieces of pottery breaking underfoot. Sometimes from a dry spot would rise the choking scent of soft, powdery ashes mixed with very fine dust.

From somewhere indistinct the moon began to shine again. The air was thick with vapor, so that in the distance the street lights shone dimly each in its individual haze. Only infrequently the stillness and the wetness were dissipated by a strong, brief gust of wind still lifting off the sea far away to the right, and then the stillness returned. At such moments the man, taking long, easy strides, took in deep breaths of the air that now fascinated him with its freedom from decay.

At the big bridge there was something that looked like a dark van with big red taillights. From the distance it had the look of a police van. As the two drew nearer they saw four figures moving here and there around it. A lorry with a very noisy exhaust passed, and they saw it stop at the bridge. It was some time before it moved off.

'Police barrier,' the man said, placing a hand on Koomson's arm. Koomson went momentarily rigid, then the knowledge seemed to have sunk at last into his confusion, leaving him walking stiffly on as before.

'This way,' the man said to his companion. But Koomson continued walking straight toward the barrier on the road ahead. Quickly, the man dropped a step down the side of the road, pulling Koomson after him. After a sharp descent the roadbed gave way to gravel and to hard, thorny grass. The man walked very slowly, taking care to keep the group at the bridge within sight. The light was not strong, but it would have been possible for any swift movement, even at a distance, to have been detected.

After the gravel there was the coarse dust before the sand, and then the sand itself. The sea waves were soft and almost noiseless, starting from far in and breaking in long, smooth lines only a few feet from the shore – small, gentle waves in the night.

Gently, the man drew his companion after him almost to the

edge of the sea, then turned left again and walked very carefully with him along the shore. As they got closer to the bridge on the left, the man stooped from time to time to pick up a pebble and throw it casually out into the sea. There was no noise at all as they passed by the bridge, only the sound of little afterwaves hitting the side of a timber log stranded on the shore. Not a single vehicle passed.

When the two reached the beginning of the breakwater the bridge itself was a small thing far behind them. Soon the huge rocks that had been thrown down on the shore for the building of the breakwater made it impossible for them to continue walking along the beach itself.

The man took hold of Koomson and helped him over the rocks to the base of the breakwater. Then, showing his companion what to do, he stooped low so that his head could not be seen from the road on the other side, and walked forward along the concrete structure. Now and then the easy sounds from the sea to the right would be crossed by harsh sounds from the road to the left of strong vehicles driven in a hurry.

The two kept their heads low, walking painfully in the curve, till the point at which the road swung away from the shore and the breakwater itself ended in a haphazard pile of leftover rocks and solidified bags of cement. Then they walked on along the shore.

Near the Anafo area the man led Koomson out first into the street and then down the small, dusty lanes of the neighborhood.

'You know the boatman's home better than I,' the man said. 'You'll have to take the lead.'

Koomson murmured weakly, then seemed to quicken his step. He led the man down a long, circuitous route, so that he was beginning to suspect that he was following a lost man. But just then he saw the low house that looked like some long thing flattened against the earth, and they walked all the way to the unpainted door at the extreme end.

Softly the man knocked on the door. Small, easy sounds inside, like the rustle of a mat disturbed.

172

'*Hei* Jack! Have you come?' the voice from inside shouted.

Koomson seemed to shrink from this human voice wanting to know who was out there, as if each sound, immediately it was uttered, had formed itself into a needle and was pricking his skin. And the man stopped himself from answering.

'Or ... Alomo, is it you?' the voice came again. 'Alomo!' After that only the silence of a baffled person inside. The man knocked again, trying to make the wood sound gentle and re-assuring. But the silence inside had become absolute.

The man bent down and said softly through the keyhole, 'Brother, come. It is nobody, just the Minister.'

Now the voice within broke its silence. 'Ah, Master, is it you?' How rapidly this voice had lost the accustomed rever-ence. There was fear in the boatman's voice still, but on this night it was not the fear of the weak confronted with the powerful. It was unmistakably the fear of one weak man in the presence of another just as weak, the potential prey of powerful enemies, and therefore a dangerous person to be with. There was a long, thoughtful pause before the boatman within opened the door and looked out at the two men.

The boatman's eyes were no longer the diffuse, vaguely pleading eyes of the hireling the man had seen the first time. Now it seemed that a certain sharpening hardness was coming into them.

'Come in.'

Was there a kind of impatience mixed with fear in the voice now? Definitely there was none of the old apology. Instead, the invitation was uttered in a manner that made it plain that the speaker knew he was doing his guests a favor.

The two men entered. Finding nothing to sit on, they stood in the middle of the little room, the boatman facing them. On the floor at his feet there was his mat, laid out for sleeping on. A chopbox made out of the pale wood of packing cases stood against the back wall. On top of it there was a pan of *gari* that seemed to have absorbed all the water in which it had been soaked, so that small bits of black charcoal grit and yellow cassava string were left above it, like stranded debris after the tide has gone back in. A long pause between them, and then the boatman began.

'Ah, as for me, I have been here. This is my humble place. It is you who have come some way. So my mouth is closed, as my ears are open, in order that I may hear what you bring with you.'

There was this boatman falling back upon the ancient dignity of formal speech. In front of him there was no longer a master, but another man needing his help. The man refrained from saying anything. It would be up to Koomson himself to frame the words to beg his servant. But Koomson hesitated, for a long time able only to look at the boatman with something like the bitterness of hate, an unspoken accusation to ingratitude in his eyes. He must have been holding in his breath for some time, for when at last he spoke, it was after letting out a huge surge of breath. And he did not speak in the manner of a master either. His voice was subdued, and his tone was much softer than that of a straight bargainer, though it had not sunk all the way to pleading.

'You know what has happened,' Koomson said.

'Yes.' The boatman's eyes were growing harder, and he smiled a little. Koomson tried to look straight into his face.

'You used to repeat a certain proverb,' said Koomson. 'When the bull grazes, the egret also eats. Do you remember?'

The boatman replied with a surly 'Yes,' as if to indicate that time and change ought to modify the truth of all such proverbs. The man, now standing a little apart from the party man and his boatman, sensed that if anything was to get said it would have to be said quickly.

'There is not much time,' he said. 'There is no time at all, in fact.'

'If you can help me,' Koomson said to the boatman, 'half the boat will be yours.'

'Where are we going?' the boatman asked.

'Will you go then?' asked Koomson.

Another grudging 'Yes.'

*

The fishing harbor was not far from the boatman's house, and they met no one on the way there, though a few times they saw people in lonely motion in the far distance, and heard indistinct voices in the night. As they came to the harbor gate the night watchman rose from his sleep and stood against their entry. The boatman seemed about to force his way in, but the night watchman took out a whistle that glinted in the yellow light and put it to his lips. He did not blow it, however, but just kept it up there, content to let it be a threat, no more. In the faint light the man could see the watchman nodding his head in amazed understanding.

'*You tink say ah no sabe,*' he said at last. '*Ah sabe. Ah sabe sey you be Nkrumah party man. You no fit pass.*'

The watchman stood barring the way. The three men stood facing him. Up the road behind them a Jeep climbed the hill leading to the old fort, and for a moment its headlights reached all the way to the harbor gate. The man saw the watchman's face in the momentary glare, and it was not the face of a man eager to make good his threat. It was the face of a man expecting something unusual to happen, some lucky chance to fall. And he, too, did not seem to notice the smell. He just stood there with his lips parted and his palms held easily in a gesture of open confidence, and the whistle dangling as if held in place by some mysterious, invisible power.

Koomson was standing like a man completety doomed, unable to help himself.

'Give him something,' the boatman said to Koomson, in an irritated voice. Like a dead man, Koomson stuck his hand in his left back pocket and pulled out his wallet. He made a motion as if he intended in his absence of mind to give the whole thing over to the watchman. The boatman, with a rapid movement, took the wallet, opened it, and for a long moment peered into it. Finally, he extracted a lone bill and held it up just in front of the night watchman's face. The watchman maintained a bargaining silence.

'Look, contrey,' the boatman said, 'fifty cedi. Fifty.'

The watchman shook his head. 'Put one more for top,' he said.

The boatman hesitated. But the man turned to him and said, 'Give it to him, if there's another one.' The boatman took out another of the notes, and the watchman took them, slowly, with something like a loving awe, so that the notes made a soft crackling noise as they rubbed against his palm.

'Pass,' said the watchman.

The three went in through the gate. Between the boats at rest the dark water of the night sea looked thick and viscous, almost solid. The boatman walked in the lead now, and his step had an unexpected sureness about it. The two men followed him past the first line of boats, at the end of which the platform of the fishing dock took a sharp-angled turn to the left. The boatman stopped at the second boat and waited for the two men to climb into it. When he himself got in he went straight to the back of the boat where the engine was, calling the man after him.

'You'll have to help me start it,' he said. 'Hold this.' He gave the man what looked like a small crankshaft, an undersized version of the things still found on old lorries. The boatman moved off a few feet and bent over something near the floor of the boat. 'Now turn it!' he shouted.

The man obeyed. It took far more effort than he had supposed at first to turn the shaft. In the darkness before him the boatman was breathing hard and audibly and making swift, shadowy motions with his hands. In another moment the engine had started, the first hesitant explosions subsiding in a smoother, more regular throbbing.

'Okay, now,' said the boatman, moving up to the front of the boat. The man followed.

The boat moved out slowly, first into the center of the dock space, then, gathering speed, it slid past the long arm of cement forming the outside breakwater and left the still, black water within it behind. The sea became something more visible as the spume began to rise in the wake of the boat, and the receding town, with its weak lights, now seemed to be something apart, something entirely separate, from the existence of the man. Further out the wake began to shine briefly with the phosphorescence of the sea, and the man leaned over and for a

176

while was able to forget everything as he looked at the strange, soft, watery light.

Then the smell of shit which had never really left him, became even stronger, and when he turned he saw Koomson next to him.

'You are going back,' the Party man said, against the engine noise.

'What will Estella do?' the man asked.

'She will be all right,' said Koomson. 'If they don't trouble her she will be all right.'

'She has enough money?'

'Uh-huh.'

'Where is she now?'

'With her mother.'

'She knows where you're going?'

'Uh-huh. Some of her relatives live in Abidjan.'

There was a long pause filled with the strange emptiness of two lives spent apart. With the increasing speed of the boat the wind grew sharper and had more of the smell and the wetness of the sea in it.

'Is there anything I can do?' the man asked.

Koomson seemed not to know, but at last he said, 'Go and see her sometime.' And then, in answer to nothing, he added, 'There are friends who will look after her.'

From out in front, the boatman shouted something that got lost in the wind around the boat and the sound of the engine. The two men moved forward.

'We are coming near Essikado,' the boatman said to the man. 'The bay is out there if you want to go down.'

Now the town looked very far away, and the man felt achingly free of everything in it.

'Yes,' he said. 'I'll go down.'

Almost immediately the boatman turned the boat so that its wake made a wide arc going first to the right and then bending left in the direction of the bay.

'There are lorry tires over there, to your right,' the boatman said. 'Take one. You'll need it to help you float to the beach.'

The man went to the pile of inner tubes and took the largest

177

and firmest he could find. When the boatman had slowed the boat down almost to a stop, the man threw his inner tube out and away from the boat, in the direction of the shore.

'You are going, then,' said Koomson, coming forward to the man.

'Yes.'

The Party man took his hand. 'Thank you.' The man heard the words, but he felt nothing for Koomson.

'We shall meet again,' Koomson said.

To the man the words sounded funny and childish, but, as if he were not himself but someone completely different, he heard himself repeating, 'We shall meet again.'

'*Yoo*, farewell!' the boatman shouted to him.

For a second the man stood at the edge of the boat. A little wave passed underneath and the thing swayed softly. The man jumped out and went down into the blackness of the water.

It was not cold. The man let himself drop deep down into the water. He stayed there as long as he could, holding his breath. He held his breath so long that he began to enjoy the almost exploding inward feeling that he was perhaps no longer alive. But then it became impossible to hold on any longer and involuntarily he gasped and let in a gulp of water that tasted unbelievably salty. The surface seemed so far up that he thought it would never come, but suddenly the pressure around his neck and in his ears was no more and he opened his eyes again. It was no longer possible for him to see the town above the curve of the water, but there was still the gently retreating sound of the boat, and when he looked harder he could make out the shape of it as it rode out at the end of its own dim wake. The man closed his eyes to get again the feel of the darkness, and then opened them.

The inner tube was farther from him than he had expected it would be. He swam up to it, ducked under and climbed up through the center with his body from the waist down still inside the water. Moving forward in the sea with slow, comfortable movements, he made for the bay.

When he reached the beach he was very tired even though his movements had been gentle, and where his upper arms had rubbed against the inner tube he felt sore in a persistent, irritating way. He had begun to feel much colder, too. But at the same time, even the cold feeling gave him a vague freedom, like the untroubled loneliness he had come to like these days, and in his mind the world was so very far away from the welcoming sand of the beach beneath him.

CHAPTER FIFTEEN

When he awoke he felt very cold in the back, though already the sun was up over the sea, its rays coming very clean and clear on the water; and the sky above all open and beautiful. A long way away a lone figure, indistinguishable at that distance, was advancing along the sand.

The man closed his eyes, but turned them directly into the sun. Colors, dark purples and orange yellows, played beneath his eyelids, escaping every so often into a vanishing darkness only to come again. When he opened his eyes fully again, the lone figure coming over the sand was closer.

It was a woman, and from the way she moved over the sand it was plain that she was mad. From time to time she stopped for long, still periods; then without hurrying at all she moved on again, frequently looking left at the sea, and less often right at the coconut trees and beyond them the green bushes along the other side of the black road.

He saw her face. It was not young, and it looked like something that had been finally destroyed a long time back. And yet he found it beautiful as he looked at it.

She came straight toward him, so directly that he was actually on the point of deceiving himself into thinking that she was about to speak to him about something he could understand. But just in front of him she stopped again, bent down to take in her hands as much of the morning sand as they could hold, and then stood up letting the sand drop fine and free through her fingers to drift away with the soft breeze in the clear sunlight. And as the sand fell she was saying with all the urgency in her diseased soul, 'They have mixed it all together! Everything! They have mixed everything. And how can I find it when they have mixed it all with so many other things?'

She stooped again, the woman looking for something lost in the sand, trying in her search to separate the grains. Her lips were parted in a smile. The man tried to return the smile, and, looking directly into her face, he called her, 'Maanan.'

The woman laughed at the name, with a recognition so remote that in the same cold moment the man was certain he had only deceived himself about it. Then she walked away toward the distant town, away from the sun with her shadow out in front of her coloring the sand, leaving the man wondering why but knowing already that he would find no answers, from her, from Teacher, or from anybody else.

The man felt something get out from him, from the endings of the nerves and the fingertips, from every part of his body, sinking into the sand. He closed his eyes again and lost himself in the dark pink shadows within.

The sun was high when he rose again. The sea looked lighter, with its greens and blues separate, not the indiscriminate dark color of the early morning. Waves, furling at the edges, came all the way and broke into little pieces each right on top of the last. The man thought of his sandals left at the bottom of the sea. His clothes were almost entirely dry now. The rubber tube was floating away to the east with the current, rising, coming forward every now and then and being sucked rapidly back then lingering until another wave took it again forward and farther to the east. The man turned away from the sea and climbed onto the coarse grass after the shore, under the coconut trees.

As he crossed the cemetery before the road, the man saw two little boys chipping pieces of marble off the headstones. They ran away as he came near, but when he walked on by they returned to the headstone they had been working at.

The road with its tar had an exciting warmth underneath the sole, but after a little distance it got too hot and the man walked on the side of it, on the brown earth and gravel.

At the town boundary, at the bottom of the Roman Catholic school up on its hills scarred with rust-red gullies, the soldiers had put a barrier across the road and were standing near it. Policemen, also carrying guns, were examining vehicles one at a time as they came up to the barrier. Cars got through quickly, but buses and trucks had to wait longer as the men and women on them were searched. Even those that had been searched were kept waiting by the roadside until a policeman or a soldier thought to come over and wave the driver on. The man stopped by the roadside, squatting in the grass to watch what was going on.

A small bus, looking very new and neat in its green paint, came up to the barrier. One of the policemen casually waved it to a stop and then just as casually he walked away to join the others. There were only a few vehicles at the barrier now, but the policemen were busy looking at a large book one of them was holding.

The driver of the small green bus stepped down and walked carefully over toward the policemen. He was young, and he was in a pair of khaki shorts, with a light green shirt over them.

'Constable,' he said, as he got to the policemen, 'my passengers. They're in a hurry.'

One of the policemen looked up and said, 'is that so?' The driver pointed to his bus.

'The people inside. They want to go,' he said.

The policeman who had spoken raised his right hand and in a slow gesture pointed to his teeth.

The man had seen this gesture before, several times. Usually, its maker would add the words, 'Even *kola* nuts can say "thanks".' This policeman, however, was saying nothing. He was leaving it entirely up to the driver to understand or to wait. The driver understood. Without waiting to be asked for it, he took out his license folder from his shirt pocket, brought out a cedi note from the same place, and stuck it in the folder. Then, with his back turned to the people waiting in the bus, the driver gave his folder, together with the bribe in it, to the policeman.

The policeman looked with long and pensive dignity at the license folder and at what was inside it. With his left hand he extracted the money, rolling it up dexterously into an easy little ball hidden in his palm, while with his right he made awkward calculating motions, as if he were involved in checking the honesty of the document he held. In a moment he walked with the driver to the bus, looked cursorily into it, then gave the all-clear. The passengers leaned back in their seats and the bus took off. The driver must have seen the silent watcher by the roadside, for, as the bus started up the road and out of the town, he smiled and waved to the man. The man watched the bus go all the way up the road and then turn and disappear around the town boundary curve. Behind it, the green paint was brightened with an inscription carefully lettered to form an oval shape:

> THE BEAUTYFUL ONES
> ARE NOT YET BORN

In the center of the oval was a single flower, solitary, unexplainable, and very beautiful.

As he got up to go back into the town he had left in the night, the man was unable to shake off the imprint of the painted words. In his mind he could see them flowing up, down, and round again. After a while the image itself of the flower in the middle disappeared, to be replaced by a single, melodious note.

Over the school latrine at the bottom of the hill a bird with a song that was strangely happy dived low and settled on the roof. The man wondered what kind of bird it could be, and what its name was. But then suddenly all his mind was consumed with thoughts of everything he was going back to – Oyo, the eyes of the children after six o'clock, the office and every day, and above all the never-ending knowledge that this aching emptiness would be all that the remainder of his own life could offer him.

He walked very slowly, going home.

THE AFRICAN WRITERS SERIES

The book you have been reading is part of Heinemann's long-established series of African and Caribbean fiction. Details of some of the other titles available in this series are given below, but for a catalogue giving information on all the titles available in this series and in the Caribbean Writers Series write to:
Heinemann International Literature and Textbooks,
Halley Court, Jordan Hill, Oxford OX2 8EJ

SYL CHENEY-COKER
The Last Harmattan of Alusine Dunbar

The first novel of this well-known poet tells the story of a Sierra Leone-like country and its pioneers seeking freedom after the American Revolution.

NADINE GORDIMER
Crimes of Conscience

A selection of short stories which vividly describe human conditions and the turmoil of a violent world outside the individual incidents, where the instability of fear and uncertainty lead unwittingly to crimes of conscience.

NGŨGĨ
Matigari

This is a moral fable telling the story of a freedom fighter and his quest for Truth and Justice. Set in the political dawn of post-independence Kenya.
'Clear, subtle, mischievous, passionate novel'. *Sunday Times*

AMECHI AKWANYA
Orimili

Set in a complex Nigerian Community that's at the point of irrevocable change, this is the story of a man's struggle to be accepted in the company of his town's elders.

SHIMMER CHINODYA
Harvest of Thorns

'Zimbabwe has fine black writers and Shimmer Chinodya is one of the best. *Harvest of Thorns* brilliantly pictures the transition between the old white dominated Southern Rhodesia, through the Bush War, to the new black regime. It is a brave book, a good strong story, and it is often very funny. People who know the country will salute its honesty, but I hope newcomers to African writing will give this book a try. They won't be disappointed.'
Doris Lessing

CHINUA ACHEBE
Things Fall Apart

This, the first title in the African Writers Series, describes how a man in the Igbo tribe of South Africa became exiled from the tribe and returned only to be forced to commit suicide to escape the results of his rash courage against the white man.

STEVE BIKO
I Write What I Like

'An impressive tribute to the depth and range of his thought, covering such diverse issues as the basic philosophy of black consciousness, Bantustans, African culture, the institutional church, and Western involvement in apartheid .'
The Catholic Herald

NELSON MANDELA
No Easy Walk to Freedom

A collection of the articles, speeches, letters and trials of the most important figure in the South African liberation struggle.

OLIVER TAMBO
Preparing for Power – Oliver Tambo Speaks

This selection of speeches, interviews and letters offers a unique insight into the ANC President's views on the history of the freedom struggle within South Africa and, of even greater importance, his vision for the future.

DORIS LESSING
The Grass is Singing

The classic murder story of the Rhodesian farmer's wife and her houseboy.